"It'll never work, Jana,"

Ben said with renewed confidence.

"Yes, it will."

Her strictly professional argument crumbled like dust the instant he dipped his head to nuzzle her ear. He slid his mouth over hers and kissed her deeply. She issued a sexy little moan and wrapped her arms around his neck. Victory had never tasted sweeter.

"Couldn't this be construed as sexual harassment?" Jana whispered.

"Nope, you kissed me back."

"I admit working together won't be easy," she said. "But I won't reassign the case. Business and pleasure can't mix—that much is obvious. Once I file my report, we'll see what happens. Agreed?"

"Agreed." He knew business and pleasure shouldn't coexist, but no way was he going to wait until she concluded her investigation to have her in his bed. In fact, Ben believed that once he proved his point— that work was nowhere near as gratifying as their mutual satisfaction—she'd wing the case off to another investigator *pronto*.

His smile widened at the thought of all the tantalizing possibilities and pleasures ahead.

Dear Reader,

When I started writing the SOME LIKE IT HOT trilogy I couldn't help but wonder if I should have my head examined. Could I really handle such a daunting task? For months I would be living with these characters and no others. By the time this month's sexy installment was near completion, I was deeply saddened to see these people leave. The Perry brothers had been with me for such a long time and were such an integral part of my writing life, it was almost impossible to say goodbye to Cale, Drew and Ben.

This month I give you *Under Fire,* and our final hero, Ben, in my sexiest Temptation novel to date. Not only do Ben and Jana heat up the pages, but Ben has definitely met his match when he's faced with someone even more strong willed than himself—the woman he learns a little too late is about to change his life.

I hope you'll join me again in December for my first novella in a very special Harlequin Blaze release, *Stroke of Midnight* (#114), a supersexy anthology with talented friends and fellow Blaze authors Carrie Alexander and Nancy Warren.

I would love to hear from you and know what you thought of the SOME LIKE IT HOT books. Please write to me at jamie@jamiedenton.net or P.O. Box 224, Mohall, ND 58761.

Happy holidays,

Jamie Denton

Books by Jamie Denton

HARLEQUIN TEMPTATION
942—SLOW BURN*
946—HEATWAVE*

*Some Like It Hot

JAMIE DENTON

UNDER FIRE

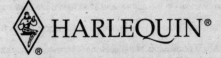

HARLEQUIN®

TORONTO • NEW YORK • LONDON
AMSTERDAM • PARIS • SYDNEY • HAMBURG
STOCKHOLM • ATHENS • TOKYO • MILAN • MADRID
PRAGUE • WARSAW • BUDAPEST • AUCKLAND

For Melissa

The joy you bring our family is truly a treasure.
You will always hold a special place in our hearts.

ISBN 0-373-69150-5

UNDER FIRE

1

"YOU'VE NEVER had a *what?*"

Jana Linney sank lower in her chair. What was the big deal? It wasn't as if she'd told her two closest friends she was a virgin, for crying out loud.

She glanced toward the back of the bar, praying the drop-dead gorgeous hunks seated around the table in the far corner of the Ivory Turtle hadn't heard Chloe Montgomery's astonished outburst. "I don't think they heard you over at the pool tables," Jana muttered.

She should have known better than to order something other than her usual glass of white wine. Bucking tradition wasn't her style, but the new case she'd been assigned prior to leaving the office for the weekend had her as tense as a bowstring. Under normal circumstances, she wouldn't sweat the assignment, but on the heels of her recent promotion, the stakes had been raised.

One glass of wine and she easily maintained and enjoyed the barest hint of a buzz. One Screaming Orgasm with an overdose of vodka and she might as well have shot herself full of sodium Pentothal. Whenever she opened her mouth tonight, just about anything came out...very personal anythings, too.

"Oh, forget the crowd at the pool tables," Lauren

Hudson, a voice-over actress, chided with a dismissive wave of her perfectly manicured hand. "I want to know how you've managed never to experience an orgasm?"

Not for lack of trying.

"I just had one." Jana giggled at her own joke. "A screaming one, too."

Lauren rolled her eyes. "Eighty-proof," she said, tapping a hot-pink, dragon-lady fingernail on the rim of Jana's glass, "does not count."

"You're not a..." A pained expression entered Chloe's lavender eyes. Today at least her eyes were lavender. Tomorrow they might be green or even a dark chocolate-brown, depending on Chloe's mood and which shade of colored contacts the corporate attorney chose to wear. "Good Lord, Jana. Please tell me you're not a virgin."

Jana sighed dramatically, then took a very long sip of her drink. She might as well have been, considering her inexperience in the sexual revolution. "I've had sex," she said defensively.

"Obviously not good sex." Lauren's bluntness usually amused Jana. Tonight that honesty irritated her. Especially since her two dearest friends were closing in on a very personal, and way too sensitive subject.

She and Lauren had been best friends since elementary school, but they hadn't met Chloe until their first year at Beverly Hills High. Since then, the three of them had formed a tight-knit circle that spanned braces, boys and good ideas gone bad which had often landed them in minor scrapes.

The sound of male laughter drew Jana's gaze back to

the group of incredibly handsome hunks at the round table near the rear of the bar. One of them stood, the one with raven-black hair, broad shoulders and lean hips. Even from a distance she could see he had the kind of body advertisers clamored for in those abs-of-granite-type commercials.

Ooh, flex for me, baby!

He glanced her way, his ice-blue gaze meeting hers for the space of a heartbeat before he said something to his buddies. Her stomach dipped and swirled, and she was pretty sure it had nothing to do with the type of alcohol she'd consumed during her Friday-night happy hour ritual with Chloe and Lauren. Unfortunately, the spell was nowhere near broken when he walked away from the table and headed in her direction.

Somewhere in the distance, she heard the rattle of Lauren's bangle bracelets followed by her perfectly pitched voice, but Mr. Tall, Dark and Wonderful had Jana's full attention as he wound his way around the crowded tables, drawing closer. He wore a dark hunter-green banded-collar shirt which clung to his wide chest, and tapered down to a flat stomach she had no trouble imagining was washboard lean. The rolled-up sleeves emphasized luscious, muscular forearms, causing her to wonder what it'd be like to have him hold her close.

He strolled past, awarding her with a view of his backside, hugged quite nicely by a pair of tan khakis. She sucked hard on her straw. The man's rear end was sheer perfection.

It was the alcohol, she reminded herself. She'd obviously had far too much to drink if she were ogling a man. Except she couldn't pass off the sudden increase in her pulse rate on a single Screaming Orgasm. She stifled a giggle. At least not from the kind served in a glass by a harried cocktail waitress.

She made a sound deceptively reminiscent of an unladylike snort. *As if I'd know the difference.*

"Earth to Jana."

Once Mr. Wonderful disappeared from her view, she turned to face Lauren. "What did you say?"

"I asked how is it you've never had an orgasm?"

"Is it really so hard to believe?" Jana set her empty glass on the damp napkin. "One—maybe even both—of you must have had sex without achieving an orgasm at least once."

Chloe laughed in that cynical way of hers, a cynicism born of being drawn to the wrong men and having her heart trampled one time too many. "If the guy's a selfish jerk or just plain lousy in bed, sure. But come on, Jana. Never?"

"What about when you're alone?" Lauren asked her.

"Alone!" She hadn't meant to sound so shocked. Really, she hadn't.

Chloe's mouth fell open and she exchanged a look with Lauren before turning her attention back to Jana. "You mean you don't even...?" Her voice faded, as if she couldn't bear to say the word.

Jana's gaze bounced between her two friends, not knowing what to say. Obviously her silence was enough of an answer for Chloe.

"I guess if you don't know what you're missing," Chloe added with a shrug, "then what's the point?"

Lauren thought about that for a minute before nodding in agreement. "You might have something there."

Jana considered signaling the waitress for another drink, but decided against it. Who knew what would come out of her mouth if she downed a second Screaming Orgasm?

"What you need is a man," Chloe proclaimed suddenly.

"She needs a *good* man." Lauren punctuated the clarification with soft laughter. "A really good man."

Jana straightened and pushed a loose strand of hair from her cheek. "A man is the last thing I need," she said, giving them both a stern look and hoping they'd take the hint.

She hadn't exactly sworn off men, but after the somewhat unpleasant end to her last relationship, she was in no great hurry to leap back inside the dating circle. Not that free-spirited Lauren or use-'em-and-abuse-'em Chloe would understand, but Jana had decided to take advantage of the emotional downtime to focus solely on her career in public administration.

Her decision had paid off, too, since she'd finally landed a promotion to supervising investigator for the Occupational Safety and Health Administration's Fire Investigation Division. Unfortunately, that meant her next assignment, scheduled to begin Monday morning, would be under close scrutiny. And just her rotten luck, she'd drawn the absolute worst possible case.

The reminder of the upcoming assignment had her signaling the waitress for another round. She usually enjoyed her job investigating industrial accidents and recommending changes that would keep employees safe from harm. Occasionally, she was called as a trial expert, and while she loved a challenge, she much preferred her work in the field. Still, she'd rather testify as an expert witness in a thousand court trials than be the unlucky OSHA investigator to draw a case involving a fatality, such as the one she'd been handed that afternoon by her supervisor. Not only did she have to face the sadness and heartbreak of a fallen firefighter, but every single OSHA investigator understood that that special brotherhood had a unique bond that was as unbendable as iron. She'd bet the crew of Station 43 would be no different, either. Gathering information surrounding the incident would be difficult under the best of circumstances. With a fatality involved, she'd have an easier time trying to walk uphill in a mud slide.

"Not a man in the relationship sense," Lauren said, drawing Jana's attention. "In the you-need-to-experience-sexual-satisfaction sense."

"Forget it." When Jana was ready, she'd find her own dates. She'd been subjected to Lauren's blind dates since high school, and she'd had enough to last her a lifetime and beyond. When it came to men, she and Lauren operated on vastly differently levels. "I think I'd rather be celibate."

"Since she doesn't have a man in her life, how do you propose she accomplish this feat?" Chloe asked.

As if on cue, Mr. Wonderful sauntered into Jana's line of vision. He stopped at the jukebox, braced his hands on the glass and bent his head to read the selections.

Like a magnet, he drew her attention and held her prisoner.

Hello, gorgeous. Care to help me solve a little problem?

"We'll find her one," Lauren announced.

That got her attention. "Are you out of your mind?"

"Wait a minute, sweetie. We're not proposing you go on the hunt for a relationship, just find a guy that knows how to...make a woman happy."

"Not we," Chloe corrected Lauren. "You."

Jana didn't care who came up with the idea, it was still nuts. "A one-night stand?"

"Sure." Lauren shrugged carelessly. "Why not?"

Jana could think of a few reasons. First, it wasn't her style. Second, it could be dangerous. Third... Her gaze slipped back to the gorgeous specimen still at the juke-box. "I don't know."

She wasn't really considering Lauren's crackpot plan, was she?

Of course not. Despite the stubborn streak that some-times got them into trouble, Linney women simply did not entertain one-night stands. They were trained in the values of appropriate ladylike behavior practically from the cradle. No wonder she'd never had an orgasm. She and her sisters had probably been sent subliminal messages while in the womb.

She allowed her gaze to slip over to him again. He re-mained in front of the jukebox, reading the music choices. Something must have stirred his interest be-cause he slipped a bill into the slot then made a selec-tion. She smiled when the first strains from one of her favorite Alan Jackson songs filtered through the speaker system. What would it be like to make love to a man who appreciated the same soulful music she did? Would he be gentle? Caring? Would he put her needs before his own?

Jana snagged the Screaming Orgasm before the waitress set it in front of her, then took a long drink. What was she thinking? Not only was the thought of a one-night stand completely foreign to her, she couldn't remember ever fantasizing about a total stranger...until *him*. In fact, now that she thought about it, she'd never fantasized about any man.

"What's to know?" Chloe slipped the waitress a twenty, then waited until she'd disappeared before continuing. "You find someone you think is attractive, you get his attention, you flirt then you seduce him right out of his B.V.D.s."

Jana zeroed in on Mr. Tall, Dark and Hunky again. What good would it do? There was probably something physically wrong with her anyway. Some sexual glitch that prevented her from experiencing the ultimate fulfillment. Or maybe, as her friends had suggested, she'd just been sleeping with the wrong men.

Oh yeah, that was it, she thought sarcastically as she downed more of her Screaming Orgasm. Although she didn't necessarily believe in all that glass-slipper propaganda, she wasn't exactly a card-carrying member of the men-are-pigs-society, either.

She'd had her share of relationships. Did it really make a difference that she could count them all on one hand, starting with the out-of-character fling she'd had with the local bad boy the summer before she left for college? The best thing she could say about her first sexual experience was that it had been over quickly. She'd been saved the humiliation of having to face Brad Hilliard again when she, Lauren and Chloe had left for Arizona State University two days later.

She'd even had a serious relationship in college. Although she rated Everett Copeland a two on the knowing-how-to-please-his-woman scale, she probably would have married him if he hadn't transferred to Florida State his senior year.

Truth be told, she was great at relationships. She'd never heard a single complaint about her own skills outside of the bedroom. The problem always started when her lover resorted to drastic measures to bring her to orgasm, then blamed her when she didn't achieve one.

She didn't think she was frigid, because she did become aroused. When it came time for the payoff, however, the big bang fizzled faster than a Fourth of July sparkler. Thanks to repeated viewings of *When Harry Met Sally* she'd learned how to fake it. Meg's character hadn't lied; a man really didn't know when a woman was putting on an act to salvage his sexual self-esteem. At least, her last two boyfriends hadn't noticed, but they had been self-absorbed types, so they probably didn't count anyway.

With her gaze still locked on the delicious-looking backside of Mr. Wonderful, she asked her friends, "How do you know if a man is going to be, you know, unselfish?"

Lauren laughed. "The size of his hands."

With the icy drink still clutched in her own hand, Jana zeroed in on the hands braced on the edge of the jukebox. They were long, lean and deeply tanned.

"I thought it was his feet," Chloe added.

Ladylike or not, Jana's curiosity got the better of her. She tipped her chair back on two legs and craned her neck to get a look at the size of his feet.

"Feet?" Lauren exclaimed.

Jana flinched and nearly toppled backward. Chloe steadied her, saving her from an incredibly embarrassing moment. Nothing like falling at a man's feet, she thought.

"No way." Lauren looked over her shoulder toward the jukebox, then turned to Chloe and smiled. "Terrance wore size-fifteen shoes," she said. "Trust me, it's the size of his hands. From the base of his palm to the tip of his middle finger."

With a mountain of willpower, Jana refused to look in the direction of the jukebox again, although she was dying to see for herself the length of the man's hand.

"I always thought it was in the way he treated a woman," Jana mused. "You know, kind, gentle and sensitive to a woman's needs in bed."

Chloe lifted an arched eyebrow. "You want a real man in your bed, or Richard Simmons?"

"At least Richard Simmons would care about your feelings," Jana muttered, then took one last sip of her drink before setting it aside.

"Forget feelings," Chloe told her sagely. "It's pleasuring your body that counts in a one-night stand."

Lauren braced her elbow on the table and propped her chin in her palm. "Some men are just better lovers."

"But how do you *know?*" Jana turned slightly in her chair. "What about him?" she asked, inclining her head slightly in *his* direction. "Would he be...?"

"Good in bed?" Chloe finished for her.

Jana nodded.

Lauren shot Chloe a sly glance, then grinned at Jana. "Why don't you go find out?"

Jana coughed. Good thing she hadn't been inhaling more of her drink, else her friends would've gotten a vodka, triple sec and whatever else shower. "You're kidding, right?"

"No." Lauren shook her head. Under the brightly colored lights of the Ivory Turtle, Lauren's platinum curls were a neon rainbow of color. "I'm not kidding. Why don't you go over there and ask him?"

Jana couldn't say what exactly had gotten into her, although she was highly suspicious it was the amount of alcohol she'd consumed. "I could, you know. If I was interested. Only I'm not."

Chloe arched that brow again. "Sure you're not. And you didn't practically fall on your back trying to get a look at his butt, either, right?"

"I was not looking at his...at his behind. I was attempting to gauge the size of his feet."

"See?" Lauren said, sounding way too chipper for Jana's peace of mind. "I knew you were interested."

Jana lifted her hands in defense. "Okay, okay. I admit it. He's good looking." *Understatement of the century.*

"That doesn't mean I want to go to bed with him. I don't even know the man."

"That's the point of a one-night stand, Jana," Chloe spoke slowly, as if Jana were mentally challenged. Sexually challenged, yes. That she couldn't deny.

"It's only supposed to be about sex," Lauren added.

Chloe grinned. "Stress-free sex."

"Tension-relieving sex," Lauren threw in and laughed.

He made another selection from the jukebox. "Hot sex," Jana whispered as she envisioned his hands undressing her, gliding over her body. Lack of personal experience at fantasizing prevented her from taking the fantasy all the way. Oh, and how she wanted to actually go there and experience being swept away into a wild vortex of intense pleasure.

"Too bad you're not interested," Lauren said. "He looks like he'd be *real* good, too."

Jana frowned and turned to look at her friend. She moved a tad too quickly and the room tilted for a split second before righting itself again. "What do you mean he looks like he'd be *real* good?"

Lauren shrugged. "He's got the look. Doesn't he, Chloe?"

Chloe reached for her drink and looked in his direction. "Hmm," she practically purred. "Absolutely." The lazy Southern drawl she usually tried to mask suddenly became more prominent.

"Back off, Scarlett," Jana warned good-naturedly. "I saw him first."

"Then do something about it," Chloe told her. "For

once in your life, let your hair down and enjoy yourself.''

''I enjoy myself,'' Jana tried to sound convincing.

''If you did, we wouldn't be having this conversation,'' Lauren reminded her. ''Go for it, Jana.''

Jana glanced his way again. Boy, was she ever tempted. But... ''What do I say? 'Hey there, handsome. Wanna go somewhere quiet and turn up the heat?' Tacky.''

She'd definitely had too much to drink, otherwise she'd never consider actually approaching a total stranger, no matter how sexually intriguing she found him.

Chloe let out a sigh filled with exasperation. ''I told you, get his attention, flirt and just be receptive to whatever might happen next.''

Lauren leaned forward. ''If he's interested, he might even make the first move.''

''If he doesn't,'' Chloe added, ''then it's up to you.''

Jana reached for her drink and downed a healthy dose of courage. She set the glass down with a bang, having every intention of making a grand exit from the table.

She didn't move. As much as she would like to, picking up strange men in a bar simply didn't compute. ''I can't.''

A sly smile curved Chloe's lips. ''I dare you, Jana.''

Jana groaned. She hated this game. She really did. Whenever she was foolish enough to rise to one of Chloe's or Lauren's challenges, nine times out of ten Jana ended up regretting her own stubborn nature. Ladylike behavior or not, the one thing she'd never been able to resist was a dare. She had a two-inch scar from stitches on her backside as proof of her foolishness from the time her older sister Caroline had dared her to sneak out one night for a party they'd been forbidden to attend. They'd jumped a fence, and Jana's shorts had caught on a loose wire that had penetrated the material and pierced her rear end.

Lauren leaned back and folded her arms. "I double dare you."

"Don't do this to me," Jana warned.

Not to be outdone, Chloe ignored the warning and taunted her, "I triple, double-dog dare you."

Everybody knew you couldn't ignore a triple, double-dog dare. Doing so went against everything that was holy.

"Fine. You win." Jana stood abruptly. "I'll go talk to him, but that's all I'm going to do." Dare or no dare, she was not going to approach the man and ask him to be the next notch on her lipstick case. She made a quick adjustment to the brown leather belt cinched at her waist before she smoothed her hands down her slim, olive-green linen skirt.

Lauren stood, her bracelets rattling as she quickly undid the top three buttons of Jana's blouse, revealing more than a hint of cleavage. "Now you're ready," she proclaimed with enough authority Jana didn't dare close the buttons.

"Go," Chloe ordered.

Jana spun around toward the jukebox. Mr. Wonderful turned at the same time. Their eyes met and held.

Once again, her stomach dipped and swirled. Her palms started to sweat and her heart beat a frantic pace in her chest.

The barest hint of a smile tilted the corner of his mouth.

It was all the invitation she needed.

2

IF THERE WAS one thing Ben Perry didn't need tonight, it was the attention of a woman. Unfortunately his steadily rising testosterone had given him other ideas the minute he saw a stunning, slender blonde with a body that put air-brushed supermodels to shame, headed straight for him.

Big, mesmerizing eyes, the color of rich jade, held his gaze with a determination and intensity that snared not only his attention, but jolted his libido with the force of a bolt of lightning. Before he had time to consider the consequences, he made the drastic error of encouraging her with a smile.

He stood in the middle of the crowded bar as if he'd been planted there, unable to look away as she neared. The teasing grin curved her full lips. She had the kind of mouth destined to stir a man's erotic fantasies.

Okay, so a beautiful, intoxicating woman sparked his interest. A lot. That didn't mean he had to act on the impulse. He hadn't come to the Ivory Turtle looking for some fun for the night. In fact, he wouldn't have come at all if Scorch and Brady hadn't hijacked his pickup truck. Although he deeply appreciated their show of support after the emotionally charged week they'd all been through, he would've much rather spent the night alone in his quiet beach house.

He wasn't like them; he didn't feel the need to raise a little hell in a desperate reaffirmation of life in the face of tragedy. They all knew the dangers of the job, accepting and facing them on a daily basis. Despite stringent safety measures, accidents still occurred. The bitch of it was, this one had happened on his watch, to one of his men.

The blonde closed in on him, granting him the opportunity of an enlightening inspection. She was tall, more willowy than his first impression of her, with gentle curves and an intriguing sway of her hips as she walked purposely toward him. She was dressed conservatively for a Friday night, at least compared to ninety percent of the other female patrons. Her sleeveless blouse showed off the remnants of a summer tan and was tucked into a long straight skirt that fell just past her calves, shielding her legs from view. That didn't stop his testosterone-induced imagination from running just a tad on the wild side. Sensible low-heeled brown pumps covered her feet, rather than the pair of CFM heels conjured by his wicked imagination.

She stopped in front of him, and her smile faltered slightly. Despite her height, the top of her head barely reached past his shoulders. He waited, wondering what kind of line she'd attempt to hand him, or if she had some unique approach to picking up guys in a bar. Not that he had anything against a woman who knew what she wanted, *if* he was in the market, which he wasn't. Not by a long shot.

"I hope this isn't too clichéd." Her silky, smooth voice was confident, belying the slight frown tugging her honey-blond eyebrows downward in a show of apprehension. "But, would you allow me to buy you a drink?"

His standard reply, a polite, *thanks, but no thanks,* hovered on his lips, until she cast a nervous glance over her shoulder. He looked over the top of her head to the other two women he'd spotted at her table earlier on his way to the men's room. The flamboyantly dressed platinum blonde gave her an enthusiastic thumbs-up, while the other, a cooler-looking brunette dressed in a jewel-toned silk blouse and dark slacks, crossed her arms and arched her brow in apparent skepticism.

He didn't need to be a rocket scientist to figure out what was going on. Obviously, she'd either been coerced by her friends to approach him, or she was making good on some bet. Considering he'd been in on the giving end of similar antics himself, the signs were easy to spot.

The blonde turned to face him again, her apprehension clearly tangible now. She smoothed her palms down her slim skirt, then balled her delicate hands into tight fists. "You'd really be helping me out if you said yes."

He'd reached his self-imposed two-drink limit over an hour ago, and quite honestly, was more than ready to go home for the night. Out of the corner of his eye, he caught sight of his brother Drew, just as he nudged Tom "Scorch" McDonough hard in the ribs, then pointed in his direction. Scorch had the audacity to whistle.

Just great, Ben thought. Could his timing be any more rotten? In no mood for the good-natured ribbing they'd surely hammer him with when he returned to their table if he blew off the blonde, he weighed his options. His youngest brother, Drew, would no doubt be the worst offender. Ever since he had surprised everyone by becoming involved in an actual monogamous relationship, the constant reminders of Ben's sorry excuse for a love life had tripled, and had become twice as irritating. Even his other brother, Cale, and his new sister-in-law had begun to chide him gently about his single status, and they'd only returned from their honeymoon two days ago.

Against his better judgment, Ben decided a harmless drink with a beautiful woman was the lesser evil. Anything was better than being ragged on by the guys for allowing a looker like the one standing in front of him to slip through his fingers.

"Did you win or lose?" he asked her.

She tilted her head. A stray wisp of light-blond hair slid from the clawlike contraption holding her hair in place and brushed against her cheek. "Excuse me?"

"The bet with your friends," he added with an inclination of his head in their direction. "Am I the prize or the parting gift?"

Her wide, kissable-looking mouth split into a full grin and she laughed, the sound warm and inviting. "You would definitely be the prize. Except it wasn't exactly a bet."

"No?" Damn, she intrigued him. Not a good sign.

"How about I buy you that drink and tell you about it?" she suggested.

He had nowhere in particular to go besides home, where he'd sit in the quiet, mulling the incident over and over in his mind, dissecting each and every move he and the others had made once they'd arrived on the scene. Nothing would change. The end result would remain the same, and he'd still have to come to terms with the probability that he could very well be the one solely responsible for the death of Ivan "Fitz" Fitzpatrick.

Suddenly, being alone held about as much appeal as a root canal. "Sure," he heard himself saying. "Why not?"

Her eyes brightened considerably, as did her smile. "Jana," she offered by way of introduction, then extended her right hand.

He clasped her small hand in his, impressed by the confident strength in her grip. "Ben." No last names, he thought. Nothing too personal, which managed to convince him she wanted nothing more than to satisfy whatever wager she'd made or lost to her friends.

Her high-voltage smile faltered for a brief instant, and she pulled her hand away. "We're in luck," she said, indicating an empty booth.

Thankfully they'd be far enough away from his pals so she couldn't discern their ribald comments or witness their raucous behavior. Not that he could blame them. It wasn't every day he fell victim to a come-on by a beautiful woman.

He'd always had plenty of offers, he'd just never

been all that good at lasting relationships. He dated, if a woman interested him enough to ask her out, but eventually they all moved on once they realized he wasn't looking for emotional intimacy.

He had his reasons, and in his opinion, they were valid. After his mother had died when he was only ten years old, Ben had witnessed his father's slow deterioration. Assuming the care of his younger brothers and attempting to shield them from the old man's self-destruction had been tough, but he had learned a valuable lesson and had sworn he wouldn't be like his father. Ben had been in his teens when he'd realized he had more in common with his mother, a woman who hadn't allowed anything to interfere with what was really important to her. Something his father had resented so deeply he'd let it destroy him.

Physical intimacy, however, was another matter altogether, and had never been a problem in his opinion. In his experience with women, most of them wanted what he refused to give them—a commitment. His last girlfriend had accused him of being emotionally bankrupt because he hadn't allowed her to clutter up his home with her personal things.

He caught the waitress's attention as Jana slid into the booth. One drink, he told himself, then he'd thank her and leave. Granted, his body might be responding to the awareness starting to take hold, but just because she'd approached him didn't necessarily translate to her wanting more.

More male laughter rose above the din, causing him to glance over his shoulder to the round table in the corner. Sure enough, his brother and friends were roaring with laughter. Ben didn't care much one way or the other if they'd made him the butt of one of their jokes. They needed to blow off steam after the day they'd had. If he was the punch line, then he figured that was the least he could do for them.

JANA TOOK a slow, even breath in a vain attempt to convince her insides to stop jumping with nervousness. The hard part was over, and she had nothing to worry about—she hoped.

She smoothed her moist palms down her skirt again. All she had to do was get through one drink without making a total fool of herself. After a little inane, meaningless conversation, she'd hightail it to the relative safety of Chloe and Lauren and lie through her teeth that Mr. Wonderful was either too dull or gay.

So then why could she still feel the touch of Ben's hand over hers? And what was with the electrifying warmth uncurling in her belly? All because she'd shaken his hand? Ridiculous. And tempting beyond belief.

"What about your friends?" she asked him as he slid into the booth opposite her.

He smiled, and the corners of his eyes crinkled slightly. "They're big boys," he said with a chuckle. "I think they can figure it out for themselves, don't you?"

Another round of raucous male laughter drifted toward them. Her mind took a definite left turn down a treacherous path as she imagined exactly what had been so uproariously funny. To her dismay, she felt heat creep up her neck and settle in her cheeks. "Yes, I imagine they can."

Oh yes. She most definitely could imagine what they'd said, and couldn't help the wave of embarrassment rising to the surface and nearly strangling her with dread. Dare or no dare, she couldn't go through with it.

She inched toward the edge of the booth, preparing to make her escape before she humiliated herself further. "Maybe this wasn't such a good idea," she said, trying to keep the edge of panic from her voice. "I'm sorry."

"Wait!" The urgent tone of his voice stopped her, but he still reached over the table and grabbed her arm before she slipped away.

"Don't go," he said, gentling his tone as he released her. "It's okay. You don't normally do this sort of thing, do you?"

She wanted to ignore the sparks skittering along the surface of her skin from his touch, but failed miserably. Her insides tingled, too, with acute awareness. When was the last time something like *that* had happened to her? Not in recent memory, of that she was dead certain.

"You mean pick up men in bars?" The laugh she managed sounded more caustic than casual, but she slid back to the center of the booth anyway. Apparently women were as ruled by their hormones as men were. "That obvious, huh?"

"A little," he said with a confirming nod and a smile that reached his eyes, yet failed to chase away the shadows she suddenly sensed lurking there. "So why did you?"

A waitress appeared to take their order. Since Jana had bucked tradition enough for one night, she decided on a safe glass of chardonnay. "A dare," she said, once Ben placed his order for a beer.

He settled back against the imitation leather booth. The laugh lines bracketing his eyes deepened, as did his smile. "A dare?"

"Yes," she admitted sheepishly. "A triple, double-dog dare."

His robust laughter salved her badly dented pride. "I haven't heard that one since I was a kid."

"Yes, well, no one ever said grown women had to behave rationally or exhibit maturity at all times."

"That's still tough, though, even at the ripe old age of..."

"Twenty-seven," she told him, wishing she had as smooth a method for him to reveal his age. She figured he couldn't be much older than thirty-two or three.

He leaned forward and folded his arms on the tabletop, the smile still lingering on his handsome face. "Everybody knows you can't back off from a triple, double-dog dare."

"Exactly," she said, relaxing somewhat. "Chloe and Lauren weren't playing fair, but I had no choice."

"Of course you didn't. Your reputation was under fire."

Jana reached into her purse for her wallet when their drink order arrived. "I'm so relieved you understand," she said, paying the waitress.

He waited until they were alone, then asked, "Why did your friends feel they had to resort to such drastic measures?"

Because she'd found him incredibly attractive, and if her friends hadn't dared her, she never would've approached him. Because now that Lauren and Chloe knew the truth, they'd stop at nothing to see she became one of the sexually enlightened. Because she really did want to see the size of his hands for herself.

"Ah, now if I told you that," she hedged, "then I'd be putting the feminine mystique in jeopardy."

"Risk it."

Those two words, combined with the pure male interest in his magnetic gaze, had the power to send her into sensory overload, effectively obliterating her common sense in the process. "We were discussing orgasms."

"I'm intrigued," he said slowly. The deep, rich, velvety smooth tone of his voice made her think of whispered words lovers shared after midnight. *Sated* lovers.

She wished.

"I suppose now I have to explain why we were discussing orgasms?" *From this day forward, nothing but a single glass of house wine—preferably white and boring—will ever pass my lips.*

He shrugged his big, wide shoulders, and Jana reached for her wineglass, reminding herself not to gulp the contents. "I really should've ordered coffee." She drained a third of her glass in one swallow. Forget name, rank and serial number. If she had the keys to Fort Knox, she'd hand them over.

"Because I've never had one," she admitted, and she didn't even blush.

Much.

Ben nearly choked on his beer. He stared at her long and hard, struggling to comprehend her outrageous statement. "You're a virgin?"

"Oh, for heaven's sake," she blurted. "No. I've just never..." She shrugged. "You know."

Heaven help him, he still couldn't believe what he'd just heard. In fact, he couldn't believe she'd told him something so intensely personal. He had a million questions, but only one managed to get past his shocked-to-the-core mind. "Why not?"

She let out a sigh. "If I had the answer to that, then we probably wouldn't be sitting here because there'd have been no need for Chloe and Lauren to issue that stupid dare."

"Can I ask exactly what this dare consisted of?" An endless stream of sensual possibilities swamped him, all of which concluded with him, Jana, tangled sheets and bodies glistening from exertion—sexual exertion.

Her big green eyes widened. "Oh! No. Not that," she said quickly. "Your virtue is perfectly safe with me."

Disappointment nudged him. Especially with that tangled-sheet fantasy still going strong.

"So. Ben." She made a huge production out of folding her napkin into a small triangular shape. "What is it you do for a living?"

"I think I'd rather hear you talk about orgasms."

She reached for her wine, her slender fingers wrapping around the tall, slim glass.

He shifted in his seat.

"That does appear to be the hot topic tonight, doesn't it?" she mused.

"It could be a very hot topic." The only thing more dangerous than lust was ego, and both of his had just redlined.

Her eyes took on a sassy glint and she raked her nails over the damp napkin she'd been folding, shredding it.

He swallowed. Hard.

"Read any good books lately?" she asked him.

"You're changing the subject."

"I'm trying to," she said, then let out another sigh. "You never did tell me what you did for a living."

He slipped his hand over hers, settling his fingers over her wrist. The rapid cadence of her pulse was a huge turn-on, not that he had far to go in that department. The night suddenly held a wealth of possibilities, and not a single one of them included him returning to his place alone for the night. He was starting to understand why people needed to reaffirm life in the face of tragedy. Maybe, for once, he could forget about being the responsible one, the one always in charge. Maybe Jana could help him forget.

"Let's not talk résumés when there are so many other interesting subjects up for discussion. Like that orgasm you've never had, for instance."

"Ooh," she practically purred. "I bet you're great at seducing women. Do you seduce a lot of women, Ben?"

He detected a hint of apprehension in her voice and understood the import of her question. "No," he told her honestly. He'd never been accused of being a player. In fact, just the opposite. "Not a lot."

The tip of her tongue slid across her bottom lip. His libido spiked.

She dropped her gaze and slowly twisted their hands until his was cradled, palm up in hers. She traced the tip of her finger over his ring finger as if feeling for an impression. She continued her inspection of his hand, spanning the length with her fingertips. A sultry smile curved her mouth. "Very impressive," she said, her voice a low, throaty whisper.

Drawing his next breath took a concentrated effort. When she lifted her gaze to his, his heart stuttered dangerously at the desire he detected in her gaze. One word from Jana was all it would take for him to open the door to a night of incredible pleasure. A night he wouldn't have to spend alone with his own miserable hide for company.

One word.

"Ben? Let's talk orgasms."

She'd just said the magic word.

3

"WHAT WOULD YOU like to know?"

Can you make the earth move?

Got any fireworks in your pocket?

Pertinent questions, Jana thought. At least in her painfully uninformed opinion. Darned appropriate, too, considering the sparks still skimming along the surface of her skin.

Risk it. Those two words held more meaning for her than Ben could possibly know.

"Well..." She drew in a deep breath, gathering more courage. "Are orgasms really everything everyone says they are?"

She hardly thought it possible to surprise him more than she already had with her earlier admission, but obviously the feminine mystique was hardly in danger. Not if she used the distinct hike of his eyebrows and the curiosity filling his pale-blue eyes as a barometer.

He took a long, slow drink from the amber bottle of beer clutched in his hand. "You seriously don't know?" he finally asked. A dark lock fell across his forehead and he rammed his fingers through his hair to push it back in place. His hand stilled at the back of his neck a moment before dropping to the table.

She shook her head and twirled the stem of her wine-glass. "Nope."

"Not close?" His long fingers flexed, tightening around the bottle. "Not even once?"

Did he have to sound so shocked? "Well..." She considered her answer for a moment. "Maybe. Once." She shook her head. "No. On second thought, I don't think it was the real thing."

He stared at her with that intense, icy gaze, as if she'd just spoken in a foreign language.

"You don't *think?*" He laughed. Full, robust laughter that made her smile despite the difficulty she was having discussing her malfunctioning G-spot. "This I do have to hear."

She held up her index finger and gave him a look of mock sternness. "Hold it a minute. I thought I was the one supposed to be asking the questions here?"

His grin deepened. "Yeah, but your answers to mine are very interesting."

"More like embarrassing," she muttered, then took a sip of her wine.

His expression sobered. "Don't be embarrassed, Jana. Inexperience is nothing to be ashamed of."

She set her glass on the damp napkin. "I never said I was inexperienced. There's a difference."

"Not if you've never had an orgasm," he said as he leaned forward. "Your lovers must've been damned selfish."

She cleared her throat. A sharp stab of self-consciousness pierced her, then she quickly chastised herself for being so silly. Ben was absolutely right. Why should she be embarrassed by their conversation or because she'd had lousy lovers? Tonight, she could say or do anything. It wasn't as if she'd ever see him again.

"You must find this all very entertaining," she said.

The color of his eyes deepened to the color of the ocean. "I have a feeling you'd be a very entertaining woman."

The air practically crackled with electricity around them at his quietly spoken words. She felt a sharp tug of desire in her abdomen. "I was thinking the same thing," she said brazenly, unable to look away. "About you."

Oh, good grief, why not just write Take Me Now, Stud on her forehead in bright red lipstick? It'd certainly be direct, but nowhere near as fun and liberating as flirting so outrageously with such a gorgeous hunk.

A slow, lazy smile curved his mouth. He had such a great-looking mouth, too, with a full bottom lip she was dying to taste.

Her breath caught, then came out in a rush. If just the thought of kissing him nearly stole her breath, she couldn't wait to see what would happen if she tried to cure her orgasm problem.

"You're evading the subject again," he teased. "Tell me how close you've been to having an orgasm."

What she wanted was to tell him exactly how close she'd like to get with him. Past the clouds. Over the moon. Fireworks, bursting stars, the whole enchilada.

Or so she'd heard.

"Jana?" he prompted.

"I felt..." The tempting quirk of his lips combined

with the husky note in his voice snatched her breath again, halting her capacity for rational thought. "Tingly," she finally blurted.

"Tingly." He repeated the word slowly, as if absorbing it with care. "Just tingly?"

She nodded. "Just tingly."

He cleared his throat, then shifted slightly in the booth, leaning forward to brace those drool-worthy forearms on the lacquered table. "Anywhere in particular?"

Moon, stars and fireworks fizzled like an interrupted daydream when her cheeks heated as if she were a teenage virgin. "Now there you go again," she chastised him. "Asking me to reveal the secrets of being a woman."

He reached across the table, peeling her fingers from the stem of the wineglass one by one. Gently, he lifted her hand to his mouth and brushed his lips across the inside of her wrist. Awareness skittered across her skin as he lightly feathered his tongue against her pulse before releasing her.

"That kind of tingly?" he asked in a voice reserved for lovers.

A jolt of electricity shot to the tips of her breasts and sizzled, warming her entire body with the heat of immediate arousal. Exactly who was seducing whom here? Forget his B.V.D.s. Her suddenly moist panties were close to becoming history.

She cleared her throat. "Those were some pretty high-grade tingles."

"So was I close?"

"You were beyond close."

Satisfaction filled his expression. She'd probably just inflated his ego, times ten, but she didn't care. When it came to tingles, the man was an ace.

"I'd say that narrows the field. So what exactly did you feel?"

Jana knew what she was feeling now, and she'd zipped right past tingle to outright arousal. When she'd first approached Ben, she'd had absolutely no intention of embarking upon a one-night stand. Now, she was no longer certain she possessed the willpower not to see how far this night would go.

She considered her last sexual encounter in hopes the reminder of what had never happened for her would derail her treacherous thoughts and halt their break-neck pace. It'd been nearly two months before she'd allowed the relationship to move to the next logical step. All in all, the experience had been...nice, she decided. Pleasant, even. She'd been turned on, but miles from the simmering heat Ben had managed to stir with that cute little tongue-on-the-wrist trick.

"After what you just did, I'm sure *tingly* was the wrong adjective," she finally told him. "Maybe it was closer to how your feet feel when you take your shoes off at the end of a long, hot day. You know what I mean?"

His attempt to hold back a grin was obvious, but eventually he did. "Sounds more like relief than sexual gratification to me."

She drained the last of her chardonnay, then shook her head when he attempted to signal for the waitress.

"Considering that lack of sexual gratification is under debate here, it seems appropriate. Now, will you please answer my question?"

"Which was?"

"Is it really everything everyone says it's cracked up to be?"

He settled back in the booth, looking completely at ease and oh-so-sexy. "Yeah. It really is," he said with a slight inclination of his head. "With the right person."

Dozens of erotic images cluttered her mind, each more enticing than the last. Images that all ended with three basic elements—her, Ben and the closest bed. "Tell me what it's like."

He regarded her with such close scrutiny, she started to fidget with her napkin, nearly knocking over her empty glass. She adjusted the set of her shoulders and aimed for a relaxed appearance. She almost succeeded, too, until he said, "What if I showed you instead?"

BEN TOOK the key to Jana's apartment from her and slid it into the lock. He didn't bother debating the wisdom of his decision or waste time with self-recrimination about allowing his testosterone to rule his actions. Even the twenty-minute drive from the Ivory Turtle to her place in Culver City had failed to lessen the need that had been clawing his gut since Jana had uttered those magic words—let's talk orgasms.

Although his motives weren't entirely chivalrous, he did feel a connection to Jana. Only, it existed on a level he understood and even welcomed—basic animal attraction. It'd been a long time since he'd experienced such an intense need to be with a woman. After the last few days of hell, he wasn't in the frame of mind to summon an argument for why he shouldn't exploit the sexual tension that had been simmering between them since the moment their eyes had first met.

At the very least, he had to taste her, see for himself if her lips were as soft and welcoming as he'd been imagining. And there was the issue of the near physical pain he'd been feeling since she'd slid from the seat of his pickup truck. Her long skirt had caught on the seat, hiking the length far enough upward to reveal slender calves and the barest hint of a shapely knee. Not much by way of exhibitionism, but still too incredibly sexy for him to ignore.

He unlocked the door, then turned toward her and handed her the key. The faintest hint of her unique perfume raised his awareness one more notch. His body flexed as he breathed in the exotic combination of floral and spice.

She moved in front of him to rest her back against the doorjamb. Desire brightened her gaze. Beneath the yellow glow of the light in the small alcove, he caught sight of the rapid beat of her pulse at her throat. The urge to press his lips to her delicate skin, to feel the staccato rhythm against his tongue, had him narrowing the already miniscule distance between them.

"Are you coming in?" Her husky voice, and the way her warm breath feathered against his lips, filled him with an anticipation not even a saint could ignore.

His gaze shifted from her throat to her mouth in time

to see her tongue slide invitingly across her plump bottom lip. Daring him to taste her?

"Yes," he said in response to her question. For once in his life, he refused to think about the consequences of a decision and how it would affect everyone but himself. For once, he chose to act purely on impulse. He lifted his hand to cup her cheek in his palm. "But first I'm going to kiss you."

The corner of her mouth tipped into a seductive little half smile. "I was hoping you would."

Forget hesitation. He didn't bother with a tentative brush of his lips against hers. Gentleness failed when he covered her mouth with his, applying a slight amount of pressure with his thumb against her jaw, urging her to open for him.

He slipped inside. The warm silken glide of her tongue instantly mating with his sent a blast of heat south, hardening him in a flash.

As she wrapped her arms around his neck, her purse hit the landing with a thud. The sound registered in the back of his mind. She held on tight, her gentle curves plastered against him, the swell of her breasts pressing enticingly against his chest. His hands itched to tease her nipples into tight beads. He wanted to taste the taut buds of flesh, explore them with his tongue, hear the soft, arousing moans of her pleasure.

Slowly, her knee rose, rubbing against the inside of his thigh. He nearly came out of his skin. Another three or four inches, and she'd have no doubt how much he wanted her.

The tension and events of the last few days began to

ebb slowly, quieted by the silent, sensual demands of the woman in his arms. His sexual attraction to Jana had nothing to do with blowing off steam, or even reconnecting with another human in the most basic way imaginable. What drove him to taste her more deeply, to smooth his hands over her rib cage and upward to cup the weight of her breasts in his palms, stemmed from nothing more than demanding lust.

She ended the kiss long before he was ready to let her go. Little puffs of air fanned his lips as she tried to catch her breath.

Slowly, she lowered her arms and inched away, as if needing distance. Not wanting to break contact with her, he dropped his hands to her hips, preventing a complete escape.

Her lashes fluttered, and she drew in a deep breath. "*Now* would you like to come in for a while?" The strength and surety of her voice took him by surprise. He could've sworn she'd just been gathering her courage.

"Are you sure?" She might have agreed to his suggestion they go to her place where they could be alone, but he wanted, needed, to know she understood exactly what would happen once they went inside her apartment. The kiss they'd just shared had left him with no illusions of exactly what he wanted.

She replied by reaching behind her to shove the door open in invitation. He stooped to pick up her purse then followed her inside, closing and locking the door behind him.

She stood in the middle of the room, a slight frown

tugging her eyebrows. Second thoughts? God, he hoped not. He'd never been a fan of cold showers.

A table lamp emitted a soft, buttery glow over the room from atop a square white table, flanked by a pair of blue-and-white, thick-striped chairs. He tossed her purse on the cushion of the matching sofa, then crossed the plush carpet to pull her into his arms and kiss her senseless.

Jana's brief moment of considering that she could be making an epic-quality mistake evaporated the second Ben's mouth claimed hers in another bone-melting kiss. When she'd first approached him, she honestly hadn't believed for a second she'd seriously consider a one-night stand with a man she'd just met. She couldn't decide whether she'd been stupidly naive or unconsciously determined, but before she could solve the puzzle, Ben was gently guiding her backward until her bottom came in contact with the wall.

She slid her arms around his waist, her fingers spanning his rib cage. Beneath the fabric of his shirt, the muscle in his back flexed and danced at her touch, filling her with a unique sense of feminine power, rivaled only by the heated surge of arousal that had her squeezing her thighs tightly together. The coolness of the wall against her skin conflicted with the heat his body generated. He surrounded her, filling her senses with his taste, his touch, his scent. The brush of his fingers against her stomach as his hands tugged her thin blouse from the waistband of her skirt had a pool of something she couldn't define—tension? need?—gathering in the pit of her belly.

The answer to a question she couldn't even remember no longer mattered the moment the warmth of his hands cupped her breasts. Through the lace of her bra, he dragged his thumbs rhythmically over her sensitized nipples. She moaned and tore her mouth from his, her head thumping against the wall as she arched her back, desperate for more of his touch.

"Taste me." Her harsh, whispered demand took her momentarily by surprise. She'd never been much of a talker during sex, preferring instead to communicate her needs with action. Could that have been part of her problem, she wondered?

He made a sound that rumbled up from deep in his chest, dissolving any remaining ability for coherent thought. The instant he dipped his head and gently nipped and laved the slope of her breasts, she forgot her doubts and concentrated on the urgency filling her. With agonizing slowness, he unbuttoned more of her blouse, then pushed the fabric aside until it gathered halfway down her arms. His mouth over her nipple, he suckled her through the lace. She cried out from the shock of such exquisite sensation.

Her breathing faltered, then resumed with short, hard pants. She couldn't seem to draw enough oxygen into her lungs. The world tilted. No, it spun, she decided. Spun her right off the edge of reality.

She gripped Ben's shoulders to steady herself. Too late she realized nothing could put an end to the crazy, chaotic wonder gathering with the force of storm clouds inside her.

He moved to the other breast and took her into his

mouth. Her knees threatened to buckle, and she attempted to brace herself. Only she couldn't. If she did, the incredible pleasure she felt by pressing her thighs together would end.

Ben straightened, but he didn't stop touching her. His hands slid to her throat, then up farther until he cupped her face in his work-roughened palms. The appreciative look in his eyes alone did for her what no lover had ever accomplished; it made her squirm with a need so deep every square inch of her body hummed with anticipation.

Could Chloe and Lauren have been right? Was there indeed something absolutely liberating about making love to a man for the sole purpose of experiencing pleasure? Even the way Ben looked at her, with a heady mixture of awe and desire, stripped her of her usual anxiety, and filled her with a wild, reckless sense of abandonment. Tonight, she reminded herself, had nothing to do with performance, but only with absolute pleasure and gratification.

His.

Hers.

And no regrets, regardless of the outcome.

"I'm going to taste you."

His words were an enticing integration of velvet and steel. Smooth, yet strong. Like his kisses. Or his touch. Comforting yet demanding.

"Every inch of your skin, Jana. Do you understand what I'm saying?"

4

EVERY INCH?

Jana had never hyperventilated in her life, but she supposed there really was a first time for everything. With any luck, an overload of carbon dioxide wouldn't be her only first tonight.

No. She wouldn't think about that. If she did, whatever magical, sensual spell Ben appeared to cast over her so effortlessly could easily break. Instead, she locked reality away and reached for the buttons on his shirt, pressing her lips to the warm, bare skin she exposed.

"So?" She shoved the shirt from his shoulders and down his arms, letting it drop to the floor. "What's stopping you?"

With the tip of her tongue, she traced his flattened nipple then grazed it with her teeth, wanting him to experience the same delicious sensations running rampant through her. She tasted, laved and kissed a trail down his torso. A groan erupted from deep inside him, encouraging her.

Before she managed to taste another inch of the luscious length of his athlete-strong body, his hands gripped her upper arms. He hauled her against his chest, holding her tight. His mouth covered hers, coaxing, yet demanding with a sense of urgency that she open for him. A request she wouldn't dream of denying.

Using his body to support her, he pressed her back against the wall again. His hands skimmed her breasts to settle at her waist. The hiss of leather rasped in her ears as he unfastened her belt and carefully withdrew it from the loops of her skirt.

Ultimate fulfillment might be a mystery to her, but she understood desire. She'd even delighted in the most fascinating tingles a time or two during foreplay. Yet her limited knowledge had never come close to the scrumptious way Ben was making her feel with only his caresses and kisses. Hot. Achy. Breathless. Craving what had always been elusive. An awareness so powerful, every nerve ending in her body came alive.

He unfastened the snap and zipper, then stepped back to push her skirt past her hips. The material slid down her legs like a sensuous caress to puddle at her feet. After toeing off her pumps, she kicked them and the skirt aside, then stood in front of Ben wearing only her matching white lace bra and panties, and a pair of thigh-high stockings. She'd expected to feel exposed, even a little self-conscious. The appreciation in his eyes effectively kept her doubts at bay.

"You are incredible," he said with a reverence that obliterated any final shred of common sense she might have been considering. "Absolutely incredible."

She smiled as she closed the few inches between them and leaned into him, wrapping her arms around his waist and moving her body against his. Friction, stimulated by heated male flesh and lace, rasped her nipples and sent an electric shot of warmth zinging down her spine.

Another tiny tremor shook her.

"Cold?" he asked.

She gently nipped his neck before tipping her head back to look into his eyes. "I've never been hotter."

The color of his eyes deepened. "You keep talking like that, we'll never make it to the bedroom."

She gave him the most sensual grin in her pathetically small arsenal. "Nothing says we have to *make it* in the bedroom."

With his arms around her, he slowly slid his hands beneath the elastic band of her panties to cup her bottom, drawing her even closer. "An adventurous woman. I like that."

She arched her back and pressed her fanny into the warmth of his calloused hands. "Hmm," she murmured as his fingers gently kneaded her flesh. "What else do you like?"

"Fantasies. Tell me your fantasy, Jana."

She would, if she had one to share. She'd already admitted her sexual reality was a big fat zero. Her sensual self-esteem hardly needed a reminder she lacked the imagination to even conjure a decent fantasy. "I have a better idea."

His hands inched down, moving with agonizing slowness toward her center. He dipped his head and caught the lobe of her ear gently between his teeth. "Tell me."

Hot breath caressed her ear at the same moment the

tip of his fingers brushed her moist curls in a feathery caress so light she couldn't determine reality from one of those fantasies he kept insisting she discuss. Why on earth did he expect conversation when all she could think about was the most interesting sense of acute pressure slowly building inside her that kept her pressing her body toward his gently teasing fingers?

She pulled back slightly and reached for the clip still securing her hair in place. While he watched, she carefully removed the clip, then tossed it on the carpet next to her clothes and shoes. With a slight shake of her head, she freed her hair from the knot until it fell past her shoulders. "You show me your fantasy instead," she quietly told him.

The sinfully wicked intent in his eyes had her catching her breath. "Tonight, you *are* my fantasy."

She barely had time to absorb his highly erotic statement before he took both of her hands in one of his. He effectively pinned her against the wall by raising her arms just above her head, leaving his free hand to do whatever he chose. This was, after all, his fantasy.

He traced her mouth with the tip of his finger, then dragged the pad of his thumb across her bottom lip before he gently moved downward to caress her throat. His lips touched where his fingers had been, then followed the same path as his hand. His caress and the moist heat of his mouth traveled southward, teasing the slope of her breasts, down through the valley of her cleavage.

The palm of his hand was hot against her skin, rough and calloused, yet tender and reverent in execution. He created a path of heat over her rib cage while his tongue, lips and teeth strayed to her breasts, creating more havoc with her senses.

Just when she thought she would go crazy from the need burning low in her belly, he released her hands and eased slowly to his knees. The heat of his mouth and tongue never left her skin, which had grown even tighter, hotter. She flatted her palms against the wall for support. He hooked his thumbs onto the sides of her panties and slowly pulled them from her hips, tasting the skin he exposed along the way with a veneration that had her heart squeezing just a little.

He tossed the lace panties aside, then, drew his hands upward along the backs of her legs, caressing her inner thighs. She nearly came out of her skin.

As if she were as delicate as a hothouse flower, he gently eased her legs apart. The earlier pressure returned, more forceful and twice as demanding the instant he touched her wet folds and slid his finger inside her.

Her breath caught, then expelled in a rush, carrying with it a deep moan filled with such an earthy sound, it took her by surprise. Sensation overruled thought with every stroke. All that mattered were the incredible currents of energy rippling under her skin and the demands of her body urging her onward toward...toward...

She closed her eyes and shoved reality behind the locked door again. Tonight she wanted the sensual ride to carry her as far as her body would allow her to travel.

She stopped thinking and only...felt.

The beauty of total arousal. The stroke of his fingers. Glorious tension. The press of his lips against her moist curls. Fire growing inside her. The glide of his tongue as it circled her most sensitive place.

She experienced it all and greedily wanted more.

"Don't stop," she whispered.

He expertly stoked the simmering warmth into a full-fledged inferno that made her hotter than ever before. The upsurge of the flames pushed her steadily closer to...to...

He stopped.

Her knees threatened to buckle, but his hands quickly shifted to her hips and steadied her. Her eyes flew open.

He stopped?

"No!" she cried out in protest. She reached for his shoulders, but he was already rising to his feet.

She shook her head. "No," she said again once he stood in front of her. She didn't care if she was pleading with him to finish what he'd started. How could he do this to her? She'd been so close, or at least closer than she'd ever been in her life. Dammit, she'd told him *not* to stop!

The man had the audacity to smile at her. "Why?"

Her mouth fell open and she stared at him through a half-dozen thunderous beats of her heart. "Why?" she finally parroted. Surely she didn't have to explain it to him. He couldn't possibly be that obtuse.

He nodded. "Why?"

If he stooped to pick up his shirt, she just might kick him square in the backside.

"Because!" Definitely not her most intelligent reply.

His smile deepened into a grin before he planted a hard, quick kiss on her still swollen lips. "Because you were so close to orgasm?"

She eyed him suspiciously. She had no idea what kind of game he thought he was playing with her.

One of his hands massaged her bare hip while he reached up with the other to smooth away the hair clinging to the side of her face, moist with beads of sweat. "Do you still want to know why it's everything everyone says it is?"

If he hadn't stopped, she just might have had the answer to her own burning question.

"Anticipation," he said when she remained stubbornly silent. "Not just a build-up of physical pleasure and final release, but something so intense it heightens all of your senses."

"If I was looking for intellectual stimulation, I'd read a book or attend a lecture," she complained.

"Every single nerve ending in your body comes alive until you explode," he continued as if she'd never spoken. "The languid, liquid warmth that fills you is purely physical. Seduction of the mind is just as important for complete sexual gratification. A total orgasm."

"I would've been happy with half an orgasm."

His lips twitched as he drew his hand over her shoulder and down her arm to lace their fingers together. "I could've made you come, Jana, but it would've been only physical."

"You really want to go where no man has gone before?" She managed a barely-there laugh despite the sharp edge of frustration slicing away at her sensual psyche. "In order to get there, you were supposed to stay on the south route of Pleasure Parkway. What is it with men and directions, anyway?"

He smiled, but otherwise ignored her sarcasm. She couldn't help herself. His arrogance was too sexy to ignore.

He lifted her hand to his mouth, then pulled his tingle wrist trick again. This time, she almost melted.

"I promise you," he said, his deep, rich voice a husky rumble of sin, "I will give you everything you've been missing."

"I DON'T KNOW if we'll be able to use the condoms."

If there was another woman in the world more sensual than Jana, Ben hadn't met her. Or one that was as unashamed of her body, either, for that matter. Stark-naked, she stood in the doorway between her tastefully furnished bedroom and the small bathroom, the overhead light behind her silhouetting her curves.

He'd never been more turned on, or hard. He hadn't exactly been filling her with a line of BS, but he'd intentionally brought a premature end to their lovemaking fifteen minutes ago and suggested they move to the bedroom for one simple reason—he'd been too close to losing control.

If he hadn't stopped, he was ashamed to admit even to himself that he might have made a monumental mistake and made love to her without protection. He'd been coherent enough to realize that Jana had passed the crucial point of no return and was probably not in a state of mind to object.

"Why? How old are they?" He rested his back against the padded headboard, the floral sheet draped over his lap.

She turned to the side for more light and peered at the box. The quick stream of breath she blew on the box sent a puff of dust floating in the air around her. She sneezed.

"That old, huh?" He liked the idea she'd had a box of condoms in her bathroom long enough to collect dust. Arrogance? Maybe. Had to be, he decided. Anything else defied logic.

"Six months," she said with a shrug. "Could be eight. Wanna hit that light?"

He turned on the bedside lamp, then waited for her to join him. She tossed the box of condoms in his direction; he caught it with one hand. She climbed onto the bed and straddled his hips as if she'd been doing it forever. After what they'd just done, shyness would be hypocritical.

"See if you can find an expiration date."

He set the small box on the nightstand next to the alarm clock. "They don't have the shelf life of Twinkies, but anything under a couple of years is probably safe."

Placing his hands on her bottom, he nudged her closer. "Anything else you'd like to discuss?" he asked her, although conversation landed dead last on his list of immediate priorities. Topping it was the matter of Jana's first orgasm.

In the soft, rose-colored lighting from the frilly lamp,

her green eyes sparkled with mischief as she wiggled her bottom and scooted even closer. His body flexed instantly and insistently.

She moaned softly, then moved against him. "I had a question, but it's a close second to what I'd rather experience."

Always willing to accommodate a woman's sensual demands, he moved one hand up her spine to the back of her neck, applying the slightest amount of pressure. She leaned toward him and he nuzzled the slender column of her throat.

"Tell me what you'd rather experience." He dipped his tongue inside the soft hollow at the base of her throat. She trembled in his arms.

Rising slightly on her knees, she yanked the sheet out of the way. With no barriers between them, she settled back down, her hot, moist heat brushing against the tip of his penis. A tiny cry of surprise escaped her throat. Her movements were tentative, but she shifted again. She moaned with such pure delight, he had to count to ten to maintain his control.

"I want to feel *that* way again," she said. Her hips rolled sensuously forward.

He counted to twenty.

"All tight and hot. *Way* past the tingle stage." Her breath caught, then expelled, bringing with it another soft moan of pleasure. "I want you to make me even wetter this time. Hotter."

His hips bucked as she pressed down, rubbing against his shaft. She was slick and moist, and ready to accept him inside her—physically. But he wanted more.

He wanted her mind free of everything but him and every wicked delight he planned to give to her.

Or was it his own mind he wanted free tonight?

Heat simmered in his veins. His body demanded release, moving him to the point where he didn't care much about anything except the incredibly sensual woman driving him crazy with lust.

He rolled them over until she was on her back beneath him. "I definitely aim to please," he practically growled.

He figured it wouldn't take much effort to bring her back to the brink, and from the soft whimpering ringing in his ears as he skimmed down her body with his mouth and hands, he was right. He parted her legs wide enough to taste her more deeply this time. Her hips rose, reaching instinctively for more. And he gave it to her. While using his finger, then two, to explore her, he circled his tongue over the outer opening, then laved upward to where she was the most sensitive.

Her soft whimpers turned to all-out cries as her pleasure deepened with every stroke of his fingers and tongue. She was impossibly wet, dewy with moist heat. Her body was perfectly primed for his, but although he sensed her need for release and despite his own impossibly hard erection, he wasn't willing to end her sensual journey.

Instead, he drove her higher, applying just enough pressure to make her cry out, then carefully slowing her down again. Her legs trembled. The core of her clenched his fingers, yet he still refused her the release she sought so desperately. He pushed her again, only to change the pace and bring her back toward earth before bringing her to greater heights the next time.

The waiting was killing him. His own anticipation to feel her body around his when he filled her had him damned close to the edge. Holding back was no longer an option. He quickly rolled on a condom and eased his body over hers.

Supporting his weight with his arms, he carefully lifted one of her legs and settled it over his shoulder to open her fully. Only then did he slowly ease inside her, inch by glorious inch.

"Yesssss," she hissed, as he filled her.

She lifted her hips, taking him even deeper inside. She was wet, tight and so very close. He thrust into her, over and over again, urging them both nearer to the edge. The pattern of her breathing changed, becoming louder with every stroke of their bodies. Her hands gripped the sheet and her body strained beneath him.

She made a low, keening sound that rose from deep inside her. Her body began to clench tightly around him, her muscles contracting, testing the thin thread of his control.

"Open your eyes," he ordered when her lashes fluttered closed. "Look at me, Jana."

She did, and he watched in fascination as awe and wonderment joined passion and need in the depths of her eyes. Her entire body shook with the force of her release.

"Yes," she cried out as she climaxed, her body pulsing hotly around his shaft. "Oh, Ben. *Yes.*"

The sounds of her pleasure shattered the tenuous

hold of his control. Thrusting deeply into her one last time, his own release crashed into him in a powerful wave.

Slowly, the world righted itself until he became aware of the scents and sounds around him. The musky aroma of their lovemaking. The feel of Jana's sweat-slick curves beneath him. The barely discernable sound of her crying.

He moved off her and pulled her with him, tucking her close to his side. Once she was curled against him, he reached for the sheet to cover their cooling bodies. "Jana? I'm sorry. I didn't hurt you, did I?"

"No." She sniffled. "It's just..." Her voice trailed off as a sob shook her shoulders.

Concerned, he tucked his hand beneath her chin and tipped her head back so he could look into her teary gaze still filled with surprise. "What is it?"

She gave him the tiniest of smiles. "I can't describe it. It was just so..." She let out a sigh and snuggled against him. "Incredible. Absolutely incredible."

5

DUSKY SHADES of gray and pale rose filtered through the slats of the miniblinds as Ben stood at the foot of the double bed in the early hours of pre-dawn, watching Jana sleep soundly. She lay on her side, her arms tightly hugging the pillow he'd used. The sight of her had him wavering between awe and a distinct need to escape.

The escape he understood. Welcomed, even. The awe made him nervous.

The red glow of the clock on the nightstand flickered and caught his attention. He had to go or he'd be late, but he couldn't muster up enough desire to leave her. He could only wonder why the thought of not being there when she woke irritated him. Probably because he'd made love to her twice more during the night and he still wanted more. He couldn't get enough of her.

So he had an acute case of lust for a woman so uninhibited sexually that she loved him in ways that left him with a deep craving to feel her body beneath his again.

Why's that so complicated?

He'd better get out of here, he thought. Fast. He'd already helped himself to her shower because he'd overslept, something he never did. There wasn't enough time for him to stop by his place for a change of clothes before heading into the firehouse for his twenty-four-hour shift. If he hurried, he still could make it to Trinity Station before the rest of the Saturday duty crew arrived. Especially the guys who'd been at the Ivory Turtle last night when he'd left with Jana.

Despite the threat of discovery and the risk of some hard-core ribbing a change of clothes wouldn't cure, he still didn't move. God, he wanted to stay with her. His body heated just thinking about waking her again for the sole purpose of making love to her. To hear one last time all those sexy little sounds she made when she came apart in his arms would be worth the price of being hassled by his men.

In the semidarkness, he smiled at the reminder of the cries of her pleasure. He'd given her an experience she'd never had. Over and over again.

He let out a rough sigh and rammed his fingers through his damp hair as his body tightened, hardening with renewed need for more of Jana's lovemaking. She wasn't innocent by any stretch of the imagination and had pleased him in a number of ways throughout the night. But there was still a quiet vulnerability about her that he found way too intriguing for a guy who shied away from commitment.

He was nowhere near as phobic about relationships as his youngest brother, Drew, but no way was he willing to sacrifice his bachelorhood as his now-married middle brother, Cale, had done. Ben had had lasting relationships, but marriage wasn't on his agenda. Marriage got in the way. It was a distraction he refused personally to entertain. And that was an opinion he'd learned most women disagreed with vehemently.

He "did" relationships, occasionally, but on his terms. Something else he'd learned most women vehemently disagreed with over time. Eventually they always wanted to rope him in, tie him up and keep him from what he loved—fighting fires.

Leave now, he thought. Make a clean getaway. Under no circumstances should he act on the impulse urging him to awaken the incredibly sensuous woman with her face buried in the pillow on which his scent lingered.

He circled the bed anyway. Carefully, he sat on the edge of the mattress and reached over to smooth a hank of honey-blond hair from her face. Bending down, he kissed her cheek. "Jana?"

She let out a sigh and hugged the pillow tighter. "Hmm?" she murmured.

More male pride rose up inside him. Without an ounce of doubt, he knew he was the reason she was so utterly exhausted. "I've got to go to work," he said quietly. "I'd like to see you again."

He didn't lie. Although he did wonder if some latent chivalrous gene was playing a role here. He couldn't let her think she was just a one-night stand, now could he?

"Hmm...me, too," she said sleepily. Her eyes never opened so much as a slit.

"How about an early movie tomorrow afternoon and dinner afterward?" He'd shot right past chivalrous straight into wanting to get to know her better.

"Can't," she demurred and rolled over. "Family stuff."

"I'll call you," he said, but couldn't help wondering if

she'd heard him or if she'd even recall their conversation. He grinned arrogantly. She might not remember what had just taken place, but no way in hell would she ever forget him.

After adjusting the bedclothes over her bare shoulder, he quietly walked out of the bedroom and headed for the front door. He made sure to double-check that it locked behind him, then trotted down the steps to his pickup, parked at the curb in front of the apartment complex.

By the time he climbed inside the cab of the truck, he realized he didn't have her phone number. Not only had he not thought to ask her, but he didn't even know her last name. The security gate had locked behind him, so he couldn't check her mailbox, either.

He muttered a curse and started the truck, gunning the cold engine to life. Maybe he should take it all as some sort of cosmic sign that last night was all they'd been allowed and leave well enough alone.

He scanned the building for an address. He spied the black wrought-iron numerals, then repeated the digits over and over in his mind so he wouldn't forget.

He shifted the truck into gear, hit the blinker and pulled out onto the deserted side street, double-checking the name when he reached the intersection. By the time he exited the freeway fifteen minutes later, he decided the cosmos had it wrong.

His reasons for wanting to see Jana again had nothing to do with hot sex. It'd been months since a woman had snagged his interest. That alone required further exploration. Practically demanded it, in fact.

As he pulled into the parking lot of the firehouse, he grinned. Maybe hot sex was partly responsible. Hot sex and the amazing high he got when all that passion filled her eyes as her world splintered.

Oh, yeah, he thought. *Definitely worthy of a more detailed investigation. In bed, and maybe out, too.*

JANA, Lauren and Chloe had been planning their quarterly pampering for weeks, and Jana couldn't think of a better time to be sitting in the elegant, private steam room of one of Beverly Hills' most luxurious spas. The totally relaxing and much-needed massage had been wonderful, too. Even her kinks had kinks, compliments of the most incredible night of her sexual life.

The hot steam worked wonders on the stiffness still in her legs, her inner thighs in particular. Muscles she hadn't realized existed ached. Tension, of course, was no longer an issue, thanks to Ben.

She bit back a groan of pleasure at the reminder and closed her eyes. With little effort, she imagined his hands, cupping the weight of her breasts. Could almost feel the glide of his tongue and teeth grazing her tight, sensitive nipples.

"Come on, Jana." Lauren's voice interrupted the start of a very promising fantasy. "We deserve to know something."

The three of them sat in a circle on the warm ceramic tiles. Jana adjusted the knot of the thick and fluffy pink towel secured between her breasts, then gave her two best friends a glare filled with minor disapproval. "You're lucky I'm even speaking to either one of you.

You knew I had too much to drink, yet you tossed out that dare knowing I wouldn't walk away from it."

Chloe's husky laughter filled the steam room. "From that glow in your cheeks, I guess you were in really good hands."

Oh, and what hands he'd had, too, Jana mused privately. Ben had shown her pleasures she'd never imagined possible. The man was an incredibly skillful lover, generous and completely unselfish. He'd been so in tune with her body, he'd played her like a virtuoso, knowing just where to stroke and strum for maximum pleasure.

She'd give just about anything for an encore.

"He could've been a serial killer for all you knew," Jana complained good-naturedly.

"A serial killer wouldn't have left you with that satisfied smirk you've been sporting all day," Lauren argued.

The smirk in question reappeared. "That's not the point," Jana returned.

"That's exactly the point. So..." Lauren nudged Jana with her elbow. "What happened?"

The earth moved. "He took me home." He'd taken her over the moon.

Chloe leaned forward, folding her arms over her knees. "And?" she pressed.

"Did he kiss you?" Lauren asked.

Jana cleared her throat to keep from grinning like a fool again. He'd kissed every inch of her body, just as he'd promised. He'd kissed places she'd only read about being kissed. "For starters."

"Starters? Ooh, bless your heart, do tell," Chloe's Southern accent thickened. "And, honey, don't think you can skip over a single detail."

Lauren pushed a wilting platinum curl away from her face. "I'm proud of you." Her eyes gleamed with curiosity. "Now, what happened?"

Pride had nothing to do with it, Jana thought. She had, after all, embarked upon a one-night stand with a total stranger. Not exactly her smartest decision, regardless of the outcome. She'd only been half joking when she'd said Ben could've been a serial killer. She really didn't know what had gotten into her, but once again blamed her stubborn streak and alcohol stronger than she was used to for her uncharacteristic journey into promiscuity.

Although, she silently mused, she wouldn't trade last night for anything in the world. She had, after all, had herself a real, beyond tingles orgasm.

Another grin she couldn't contain curved her lips. At least now she had more than enough firsthand experience to conjure up a hot fantasy or two.

"Did you invite him in?" Lauren asked her.

Jana nodded. "Yes."

"How long did he stay?" Chloe wanted to know.

All night long.

Jana shrugged and looked down at her feet. "For a while."

Lauren made a sound of disapproval. Not, Jana assumed, because she'd actually done something reckless and carefree, but because her friend wanted all the juicy details.

"What time did he leave?" Chloe asked, her Georgia drawl filled with skepticism.

Jana bit her lip. She had no idea. She'd been awakened by the ringing of the telephone when Chloe had called to announce she'd be at Jana's in thirty minutes. As she'd scrambled to get ready, she'd recalled wisps of a conversation. She had no clue if the images floating around in her head were real or a dream. "I'm not sure," she admitted.

"I don't believe it!" Lauren exclaimed, then squealed. "You did *it?*" She grabbed Chloe by the arm. "Do you believe this? She actually did it."

Thank heavens they'd splurged on a private steam room.

"Well?" Lauren prodded Jana with her elbow again.

Jana rolled her eyes. "Did *it?* What are we? Sixteen again?" Yes, she was stalling, but she wasn't sure about sharing such intimate details of her time with Ben, even with her two oldest friends. The night had been... special, she decided.

Chloe leaned over so far she nearly put her hand out to keep from falling off the ceramic-tiled seating area. "Well? How was he?"

Perfect, Jana thought. *Abso-freaking-lutely perfect.*

"He made the earth move, didn't he?" Lauren wanted to know.

Jana laughed, embarrassed because that's exactly what she'd been thinking.

But the earth *had* moved. Like a big seven-pointer on the Richter scale complete with enough high-impact aftershocks she'd felt them in her sleep. Ben had turned her world upside down then taken her on a flight through the galaxies into a place so blissful and heavenly she'd never wanted to come back to the solidity of earth. Just thinking about it had her wanting to book another round trip.

Lauren gave her a stern look. "You're being intentionally evasive, Jana."

"I don't think she knows how much that gives away," Chloe added.

Jana had given plenty of herself away, and heaven help her, she'd do it again in a heartbeat—with Ben. "Can't I have a private moment?"

"You gave up the right to privacy the minute you confessed," Chloe argued. "Now fess up. We have a right to know. Did you get laid or not?"

A small sigh escaped Jana's lips. She had absolutely no willpower.

"Okay," Lauren said slowly, nodding her head. "You got lucky. Exactly how lucky?"

As much as Jana would've liked to, she couldn't blame the heat of the steam room for the blush stinging her cheeks. Two pairs of eyebrows rose dramatically as Lauren and Chloe stared at her, stunned into absolute silence.

Jana's smile shifted into a full grin and she laughed. Another first—she'd just shocked the two most unflappable people she knew.

"Are you going to see him again?" Lauren asked once her temporary stupor faded.

Chloe shot Lauren an annoyed glance. "This was supposed to be a one-night stand. Why do you always want to make everything so complicated? Sex for the sake of sex is not supposed to be difficult."

Lauren turned to look at Chloe with an impatient expression of her own. "We're not all sexual revolutionaries. Some of us like the idea of having the same man in our bed more than once."

"At least I'm honest about it, Yankee," Chloe said, then smiled sweetly as she flipped Lauren the bird.

Jana gave them both a stern look, then stretched her legs out in front of her and leaned back on her hands. "As amusing as you both are, I don't feel like refereeing another civil war reenactment today." Chloe and Lauren had been arguing, albeit always in jest, since their days together in high school.

Tipping her head back and closing her eyes, Jana lifted her face toward the tiled ceiling. "I think he told me he wants to see me again," she said. "I'm not sure, but I think it was some time this morning when he left."

Chloe made a sound of disgust. "So, you had a night of fabulous sex. Big deal, Jana. It doesn't mean you should start shopping for monogrammed sheets."

Jana didn't even know Ben's last name, so she was in no peril on that score. She didn't know where he lived or what he did for a living. Not that it mattered, but it would be nice to know those details about him.

She'd estimated his age to be somewhere in his very early thirties, making him only a few years older than she. While she didn't think he was married, he could be divorced with half-a-dozen junior studs in training running around wanting to be just like their daddy.

What if he was a staunch conservative? What kind of

relationship would that be for a bleeding-heart liberal like herself?

Or a slob, she thought, horrified. Her neat-freak tendencies would scream in protest over that one.

Or worse, a chronic workaholic. That she could never tolerate. She'd watched her parents' marriage crumble because her father had never been around. It'd been a miracle he'd even shown up in court for the divorce hearings.

"No," she said after a moment. "Chloe's right. It was a one-night stand." She straightened and gave them both a steady look. "My first and my last. Besides, I wouldn't even know how to get in touch with him again."

"Directory assistance," Lauren provided helpfully.

Jana winced. "I can't."

"Sure you can," Lauren said. "You pick up the phone and dial four-one-one."

"No, I don't mean I can't, I mean I *can't*," Jana explained. "I don't know his last name."

Even sexually liberated Chloe had the decency to appear slightly stunned. "You mean you had sex with the guy, had your first mind-blowing orgasm, and you didn't even get his last name?"

"Three, actually." Jana frowned. "Maybe four." She would've had four if he hadn't stopped them the first time. "No. Definitely three."

She wasn't certain if she'd fully forgiven him for teasing her like that, but at least he hadn't lied about the anticipation. When he had finally let her fall, she'd been so overwhelmed, she'd actually wept. She'd even fallen asleep in his arms afterward, completely sated. He'd kissed her awake some time later, and they'd made love again. They'd done a slow, unhurried, seductive exploration with the end result even more earth-shattering than the first time. Later, she'd been the one to awaken him. Their mating had been wild, primal, her orgasm so powerful she'd been sure she'd literally screamed from the force of it.

Chloe snapped her fingers to get Jana's attention. "Name?"

"That wasn't exactly the subject that came up," Jana admitted sheepishly. "Look, it's not important. We had a great time, but that's all it was, okay? I'll never see him again so it's a nonissue. Now can we please change the subject? Let's dissect Lauren's career or why our darling Scarlett is such a grouch today."

"She's always a grouch." Lauren smiled suddenly. "I do have some news. You'll be happy to note that my agent left me a message that I landed a string of voice-over spots for a series of airline commercials."

Jana jumped at the opportunity for a new topic of discussion. "What about the animated feature you auditioned for last week?" she asked.

Lauren had wanted to be an actress for as long as Jana had known her. Unfortunately, Lauren froze in front of the camera, something she'd discovered after landing a sitcom very early in her career. Luckily, sound people had loved her voice. For the most part, Lauren made a decent living doing voice-over spots for thirty-second ads or documentary narrations. But Jana knew how important the audition had been to Lauren, and what landing an animated feature would do for her friend's financial security, as well as her career.

Lauren shook her head. Her wilted curls bounced like limp springs. "Not yet. My agent still hasn't heard back from the producer. Oh, it'll be three days."

Jana frowned, puzzled. Hadn't Lauren just said she'd landed a series of commercials? Depending on how many spots the advertisers were looking for, it could entail a good month or more of steady work. "It's only a three-day job?"

"Lauren." Chloe's voice was once again littered with impatience. "*What* are you talking about?"

"He'll wait three days before he calls her." Lauren spoke slowly, as if Chloe were dense.

"She's right," Chloe confirmed with a brisk inclination of her head in Lauren's direction. "It's some stupid guy rule. No matter how interested they are, they wait three days until they call you again."

Jana tilted her head back and closed her eyes again, then arched to stretch her spine, loosening more tight muscles. "I never gave him my number, either, so the point is moot. And that's all I have to say about it. The subject is now officially closed."

"Just one more question," Chloe pleaded. "Who was right. Me or Lauren?"

Jana let out a sigh. "About what?"

"Feet or hands?"

Jana burst out laughing. She straightened and lifted her hand to wiggle her fingers.

"From the base of his palm," she said with a wide grin, "to the tip of his middle finger."

6

BEN HUNG UP the phone, then slipped his credit card back inside his wallet. The clerk at the flower shop hadn't been thrilled about him placing an order without knowing Jana's full name. He also hadn't been impressed when Ben only wanted his phone number on the card. Despite all the dramatic sighs, the guy hadn't been foolish enough to refuse an order for three-dozen blush-pink roses.

Roses were a pretty old-fashioned idea, but Ben had a point to make, and in his opinion, nothing spoke louder to a woman than roses, except maybe jewelry. He didn't doubt for a second Jana wouldn't realize they were from him. The decision on whether or not they'd see each other again now belonged to her. All he'd done was send her thirty-six reminders why she should call him.

The city had been relatively calm for a Saturday, and Ben had taken advantage of the quiet by catching up on the sleep he'd missed. There'd been several paramedic runs throughout the day, keeping the two squads of medics hopping, but most of the crew had been kicking back in front of the big-screen TV in the dayroom watching the college football game once the equipment and gear checks were out of the way.

He'd managed to escape being hassled by the guys, but then, the entire house had been subdued since they'd lost Fitz in the Malibu Hills fire eight days ago. The Occupational Safety and Health Administration would be breathing down Ben's neck first thing Monday morning, too. It was standard procedure for the big boys to get involved when someone died, but Ben sure as hell wasn't looking forward to putting up with some anal, gung-ho book jock with no experience putting his butt on the line. No two burns were alike. A firefighter operated on instinct honed from years of experience and training, skills that were impossible to develop by reading a textbook.

The game failed to hold his attention, which hardly surprised him. When Jana wasn't occupying his mind, he ended up going over and over the events of the fire that had cost Fitz his life.

Anxious for a distraction, he left the dayroom and headed for the bay. Cale and Brady Kent, Cale's partner, were back from their last paramedic run, busy restocking their rig and performing equipment checks.

Ben leaned his shoulder against the open door at the back end of the ambulance. "Hell of a first day back," he said to his brother, who'd been honeymooning in the Caribbean for the last two and a half weeks.

Cale looked up from the drawer of gauze bandage supplies he'd been replenishing, his expression solemn. "Hasn't been too bad," he said meaningfully. He filled the drawer, shoved it closed, then checked the next one. He looked over at his partner. "Where are the four IV bags?"

Brady smacked his forehead with the heel of his hand. "I knew I forgot something."

"Hey, how's Elise feeling?" Ben asked as the other paramedic climbed from the rig. Brady and his wife were expecting their first kid in a few months.

"Not bad now that she's over morning sickness," Brady told him. "I was starting to feel guilty."

Brady headed off to the stockroom, leaving Ben and Cale alone. "He's been a wreck," Cale said once Brady was no longer in sight. "'Course I'd probably be spooked, too, if it was Amanda bowing to the porcelain god twenty-four-seven."

Ben didn't doubt it for a second, either. He had a feeling Cale would find out for himself soon enough. He almost pitied his sister-in-law. Knowing Cale and his big old soft heart, he'd probably end up suffering right along with Amanda, and she'd be the one taking care of him.

Definitely not something Ben ever cared to experience firsthand. What real knowledge he did have about pregnancy and childbirth stemmed from the job. He'd been around enough roadside births to understand labor was no picnic—for either parent.

Cale cleared his throat. "You're looking a little ragged around the edges. Late night?"

Ben wasn't fooled by Cale's feigned innocence. "Word travels fast."

"When old boring Ben gets picked up by a hottie, there's gonna be some talk."

"Gossip is an ignorant pastime for the small-minded."

Cale shrugged his shoulders and grinned. "It's usually more interesting than the truth. So you gonna fess up or what?"

Ben moved out of the way as Brady headed across the bay toward them, his arms weighed down with several boxes of supplies.

"Didn't plan to," Ben said.

Cale took the boxes from Brady and set them on the gurney beside him. "Drew and I never plan to, either, but you always seem to get it out of us."

Once Brady climbed back inside the rig, Ben crossed his arms and propped his shoulder against the open door again. "That's because I'm smarter, older and better looking."

Cale grinned, then shook his head. "Naaah. Older, I'll give you. So, what gives?"

He supposed Cale's third degree was to be expected. And deserved. But that didn't mean he had any intention of spilling his guts the way his brothers did when he pressed them for information. Ben knew they thought he was nosy and bossy, but he cared about them. Drew and Cale were his family. He'd been looking after them since he was ten years old. Surely they didn't expect him to stop now that they were all grown up.

"Not much," Ben said, careful to keep his expression neutral. "I met someone. We had a good time." A time he wouldn't mind repeating. Often.

Cale shoved the handful of IV bags at Brady. "Did you catch that?" he asked his partner.

"Sure did," Brady chuckled. "He's interested."

Ben straightened and stuffed his hands in the front pockets of his uniform trousers. "How'd you two geniuses draw that conclusion?"

"Three missing words," Cale said, lifting three fingers for emphasis. *"End. Of. Story."* He looked at Brady. "Did you hear him say 'end of story'?"

Brady shook his head as he stuffed the drawer with IV kits. "Nope. I didn't hear it."

Cale hopped to the ground. "You're interested." He reached for the extra boxes Brady had retrieved. "Admit it."

Ben shrugged, not sure what he felt other than a desperate need to have Jana's body beneath his again. Soon.

"First you," Brady said to Cale as he followed him out of the rig, "then Drew, now Ben. The Perry men are sinking fast."

Ben took several steps back. "Whoa, hold it right there." The distance did nothing to stop warning signals from going off in his head. He was not sinking. He wouldn't allow himself to fall victim to whatever bug had bitten Cale, and possibly even Drew. "We had a good time. That's it."

That's all Jana would ever be to him—a good time—for as long as she'd tolerate him. He was interested, but what guy wouldn't be after a night of fantastic sex with a woman like her? He'd decided a whole lot of years ago he'd never let anyone or anything come between him and what he loved, and Jana would not be the exception.

After his mom, a firefighter, had died in the line of

duty, he'd watched his old man throw everything that should have mattered away: his own career as a fire-fighter, his sons, even his own life.

During those first few months, Ben had feared his fa-ther and his rages. Morbid reflection usually followed until Alex Perry would finally pass out in a drunken stupor. It hadn't taken long for Ben's fear to turn into disgust. In his opinion, every time his dad had dived into a bottle of booze, which had been often, he'd dese-crated the memory of Joanna Perry.

Cale and Drew had been too young at the time, Ben figured, to remember, or even know about, the fights his folks had had over his mom's career choice. She'd been tough and hadn't backed down from the old man or the department when they attempted to stick her in an EMT position. She'd died a hero, and as far as Ben was concerned, when she'd been alive, she'd deserved better than the guilt trip the old man had continually hurled at her for fighting for what she wanted.

"Yo, Ben. Ben!"

Ben shook off the past, just as he'd done for the last twenty-some years whenever the memories had threat-ened to choke him. He looked at his brother and at the deep frown on a face very much like his own.

Cale inclined his head toward Brady. "What did he mean 'then Drew'?"

Brady groaned and dropped his head. "Forget I said anything."

"What's he talking about?" Cale asked Ben.

"Emily Dugan," Ben reminded him. He'd suspected something was going on with Drew and Emily when

Drew had invited her to Cale's wedding. "It could be serious."

"Drew?" Cale laughed, then made a production out of grabbing his chest and stumbling around the bay. "The one with the revolving bedroom door? *That* Drew?"

Ben hadn't been half as surprised by the news as Cale, but then Ben was nowhere near as distracted as Cale had been since Amanda. "One and the same."

Cale let out a low whistle. "Well, I'll be damned."

Brady sat on the rear bumper of the rig. "He's got it bad, too."

Cale shook his head in denial. "No way. Not Drew," he said with a hearty laugh. "Women are his hobby. Remember the time he screwed up and had two of them show up at his place at the same time?"

Brady grinned and wiggled his thick eyebrows. "Yeah, and they both stayed. Some guys have all the luck."

"Not lately," Ben told them. "Since Emily, I don't think Drew's seen anyone else."

Brady rested his hands on his legs and nodded in agreement. "I heard he never even dated those couple of weeks when he and Emily weren't talking to each other."

Cale raked his fingers through his hair. "A lot can happen in three weeks."

Ben crossed his arms and gave Brady a hard stare. "What do you know?"

Brady lifted his hands in defeat. "Talk to Drew."

Cale moved in next to Ben, and they faced Brady in a united front. "We're talking to you."

"Aw, man," Brady complained. "Come on, guys. Scorch made me swear."

"I swear I'm going to pound you into the ground if you don't spill it," Cale told Brady. He wouldn't, but the threat still had Ben's lips twitching as he struggled to hold back a smile.

"Okay. Okay." At least Cale's partner knew a losing battle when he saw one. "But I'm only talking because we're partners and I have to work with you."

Cale frowned. "Get to the point, Brady."

"Scorch told me that Drew asked Tilly if she'd take him to see her jeweler today." Brady looked from Cale to Ben.

Ben shrugged, unconcerned. "Could be anything."

Brady slowly shook his head. "No, dude. He's looking for a rock."

The news took him by complete surprise. Sure, Drew had a thing for Emily. Ben didn't really know her, but she was eons away from Drew's usual type. His youngest brother wouldn't actually torch his little black book, would he? "You don't think he'll really marry her, do you?" he asked Cale.

His brother rolled his eyes. "I realize this is virgin territory for you, old man, but for somebody that claims to be smarter, you sure are dumb."

"She's pregnant, Cale," Ben said. He simply could not wrap his mind around the idea of Drew becoming a family man. The concept of commitment was foreign to his little brother.

Cale frowned. "Yeah, so?"

"So it's not his baby. Why would he want that responsibility?" Ben argued. Drew lacked Cale's hero gene. He didn't rescue women the way Cale did; he collected them. Imagining Drew dating one woman exclusively was difficult enough to digest, but marrying one who came with a ready-made family?

"Why should it make a difference?"

Ben thought about that for a moment. Maybe it didn't have to matter. The fact that his youngest brother was happy should be most important. With Cale married and Drew apparently dangling on the cusp of wedlock, Ben supposed his job was done.

"I guess it doesn't," he said eventually. Although he still wasn't sure what he thought about the commitment virus infecting both of his brothers.

"Right. And before you start poking around," Cale said, "let's go torture Scorch for a while."

"Why?" Ben asked, frowning. "What's he done?"

If the scrawny paramedic had done anything to hurt Tilly Jensen, he'd have to answer to all three of the Perry brothers, and none of them had been shy about letting Scorch know it, either. Tilly and Drew were the same age and had been best friends ever since Drew had run over her dolls with his bike and she'd given him a black eye in return. In her early teens, she'd turned into a real pest when she'd decided she had a crush on Ben, but even her infatuation with him hadn't changed his feelings. Tilly was family, and he protected his family.

Without waiting for an explanation, Ben took off for

the dayroom, prepared to have a "chat" with Scorch to remind him to tread carefully as far as Tilly was concerned. Brady and Cale followed.

"Think he's a little thick-headed today?" Cale said to his partner, loud enough for Ben to hear.

Brady chuckled. "I think his mind is somewhere else."

"On some*one* else, you mean."

Ben turned around and blocked their path, giving them both a hard stare. "Do you clowns have a point?"

Cale looked at him as if he had as much sense as Drew. "Since when does Tilly have a jeweler?"

"Ahhh. That's better."

Jana wiggled her toes and issued another relieved sigh as she carefully set her new suede boots next to the bed to air out for the night before putting them back in the box. Never again would she equate sex to taking off a pair of shoes at the end of a long day. She knew the difference now, and they were acres apart.

She pushed off the mattress and walked across her bedroom to the dresser for her favorite pair of grungy sweats. Sitting in the center, in front of the mirror, were the roses Ben had sent yesterday. The large cut-crystal vase held three dozen of the palest shade of pink roses she'd ever seen. She breathed in deeply, inhaling the luxurious scent filling the room. Flowers from a man weren't out of the ordinary, but usually she only received them for special occasions, like her birthday.

She was thankful that she'd been alone when the flowers had been delivered. After their spa day and a late lunch, Chloe had dropped her off at the dealership to pick up her car, which she'd taken in for service, so she'd been spared another of her cynical friend's sexual revolutionary speeches and Lauren's attempts to put silly romantic notions into her head.

Ben's gift made it patently clear he wanted to see her again. Although she did appreciate his generosity, she wasn't a complete fool. She suspected his reasons had more to do with sex than wanting to get to know her.

Incredible, earth-shattering sex, but still just sex.

For as much as she truly enjoyed every moment she'd spent with him, a fling wasn't her cup of latte. She hadn't been shopping for a relationship, either, but that didn't mean she wasn't open to the possibility should the right guy come along at the right time. But Ben was not that guy. Relationships led to sex, not the other way around.

Despite her lack of illusions regarding his intentions, she couldn't be rude. She had been raised always to be polite and considerate of others. What harm could there be in calling to thank him. *Just* thank him, nothing more.

After changing clothes, she lifted the card from the plastic holder and carried it with her to the bed. She stared at the phone and bit her lip. "Willpower," she said, firmly, and snatched the cordless from the cradle and dialed his number.

He answered on the second ring. The low sexy rumble of his voice started her heart pounding.

"Hi, it's Jana," she said, aiming for calm and self-confident. Instead she got nervous and shaky.

"I was hoping I'd hear from you."

He did sound pleased that she'd called, but she didn't know him well enough to determine a come-on from genuine interest. "I was at a birthday party all day."

"Yours?"

"Ooh, that was smooth." She laughed at his attempt to garner information.

"I try," he said. "So when *is* your birthday?"

That was not the question of a man only interested in sex. Her self-restraint weakened. "If you ask me what's my sign, I'm hanging up." She heard the rustle of paper in the background. A newspaper? Probably a comic book.

"Too clichéd," he said with a hint of laughter.

"So are flowers, but they are beautiful." She flopped back against the mound of pillows. "That's why I called. Thank you, Ben."

"I like hearing you say my name."

Could be a come-on, could be flirting. *Flirting,* her conscience rallied in support.

"I especially liked the way you said it Friday night," he added.

As if she needed a reminder. She closed her eyes, then snapped them open again to escape the erotic visions. "Hmm," she murmured, starting to feel warm. Her willpower melted. "Friday night or Saturday morning?"

"Morning." His voice deepened, becoming huskier. And definitely sexier. "How about dinner?"

She sat up straight. "Now?" Was he after more of the same?

"It's not quite seven o'clock," he said. "If you've already eaten, we could meet for dessert."

And just who would be the dessert? Her pulse quickened with anticipation.

She might have already rolled over once with her legs in the air, but that didn't necessarily mean she was an easy piece. "You know, that sounds like it'd be fun, but I can't."

"Other plans?" he asked. He sounded disappointed. Because he wasn't going to get any, or because he really did want to see her?

"To be honest, I'm exhausted," she lied. She'd never been more awake. "The birthday party was for my oldest sister's twin sons. Do you have any idea how much energy a dozen five-year-old boys have? We're talking hyper-speed, and a decibel level to rival a heavy metal concert."

"I understand," he said. Did he really? Personal experience? she wondered, thinking of those half-dozen little Ben juniors she'd imagined running after him.

"How about dinner tomorrow?" he asked. "I'm off at six. Does seven work for you?"

Maybe he did really want to see her again, for all the *right* reasons. "Seven's perfect," she told him. The investigation of Trinity Station would no doubt zap every emotion in her system; it'd do her good to concentrate on something other than the assignment from hell. "The downtime will probably be just what I need after tomorrow."

"What's going on tomorrow?"

She detected genuine interest and it made her smile. "A new assignment I'm not looking forward to," she told him. "And I still haven't prepped, something I need to do tonight."

"Are you sure I can't tempt you, Jana?"

He segued expertly into seduction. Regardless of her uncertainty surrounding his motives, she was hooked. She settled against the pillows again. "A back rub and I'm yours."

"My hands are on your shoulders. Do you feel them?"

She closed her eyes, shutting out the last of her self-discipline. "Yes." Fantasies were a snap now, thanks to him.

"That's warm oil I'm using. Can you feel my hands gliding over your skin? Moving down your spine?"

She couldn't breathe.

"Lower." He paused. "And lower."

If he went another inch, she'd be in trouble. She cleared her throat.

"Just relax, Jana," he practically purred in her ear. "Relax and feel my hands spanning the curve of your hips."

She sighed audibly. Forget her hips. She knew just where she wanted his hands. Desire tugged sharp and low in her belly.

"Good night, Jana."

Her eyes flew open as she heard a click, followed by the drone of the dial tone. "Noooo," she whined. God, he'd done it to her again!

She yanked the handset away from her ear and stared at it angrily. How was she supposed to get any work done now that her body buzzed with need for someone who wasn't even there, especially now that she knew exactly what sensual delights she'd be missing?

"OVER THE NEXT few days, I'll be conducting interviews with the personnel on scene during the incident, examining equipment and observing your crew in action." Jana handed Captain Rick Baker the list she'd made last night of the squad members she wanted to interview first.

She estimated the man in charge of Station 43—appropriately referred to as Trinity Station because it shared one corner of an intersection with three churches—to be in his mid-forties. So far, he'd offered no objections to any of her requests.

"I would also appreciate it if you could arrange for the scene commander to meet me at the site tomorrow to walk me through the events."

"That would be Lieutenant Perry," the captain told her before she could look up the name again. "It shouldn't be a problem."

Obviously Captain Baker understood that OSHA wasn't the enemy. She doubted the crew of Trinity Station would be as helpful. They usually lumped OSHA personnel in the same category as snail snot.

"If Lieutenant Perry's available, I'd like to start by interviewing him."

"He is." The captain stood. "He'll provide you with whatever information you need to complete your investigation as quickly as possible. Any of my men will be available to assist you with the equipment inspections, as well."

"Thank you, Captain," she said as she stood. "I know this is a difficult time for all of you. I'm very sorry for your loss."

The captain's expression visibly tightened. He nodded his thanks, then walked toward the door of the small office. "I'll send in Lieutenant Perry. Feel free to use my office for as long as you need it."

Jana thanked him again, then lifted her briefcase and carried it with her around the desk once the door closed. She was playing a definite mind game, but if she placed herself in a position the squad recognized as one of power, she just might manage a little grudging respect. She needed every advantage possible, real or imagined.

She adjusted her short navy blazer and straightened her shoulders. The door opened, and she looked up at what had to be a walking, talking fantasy. In numb shock, she sank silently to the worn leather chair.

This couldn't be happening to her.

Ben's large body filled the doorway. Dark-blue trousers outlined his powerful thighs and long legs. The lighter blue shirt of his firefighter's uniform clung to his chest and emphasized his wide shoulders. The same shoulders she'd clung to during the throes of passion.

A deep frown creased his forehead. His pale-blue eyes filled with suspicion.

"You're Lieutenant *B.* Perry?" she asked him, still unable to comprehend how something like this could be happening to her. "You're a *firefighter?*"

"That's right," he answered slowly. "Jana, what are you doing here?"

"Oh God," she muttered miserably. She propped her elbows on the desk and let her head fall into her hands. "This can't be happening. It just can't."

The door closed with a loud thud. Or was that her heart that had just landed at her feet?

"What the hell is going on?" he demanded. Nothing about his voice reminded her of the tender, skillful lover who'd whispered hotly in her ear. There was no sign of the rich, deep husky tone capable of making her squirm from a few carefully chosen words meant to seduce.

She lifted her head. Nothing about his entire demeanor reminded her of the man who'd tilted her world and shown her the true art of sexual magic. Instead, he was cold, detached, and ticked off to the max.

She suppressed a shiver of apprehension. "I'm here to investigate the death of Ivan Fitzpatrick," she told him. "I'm with the Fire Investigation Division of the Occupational Safety and Health Administration."

He muttered a ripe, vile curse.

She nodded slowly in agreement. "Yeah," she said. "That's kinda what I was thinking, too."

7

"THIS HAS to be a bad dream."

Ben couldn't argue. When he'd walked into the captain's office, he'd been expecting an officious geek with greased-back hair and a cheap suit, not the woman he'd been anxious to seduce back into bed.

"You should have told me you worked for OSHA."

She stood, her palms slapping the desktop as she leaned forward and gave him a heated stare. Apparently she'd taken exception to the censure he'd been unable to keep from his voice. Too bad. He'd just gotten the shock of his life. He'd earned the right to be uncharitable.

"You say that as if I knew who you were," she accused. "We didn't tell each other our last names, remember?"

How could he forget? He'd been too enticed by the lure of anonymity. He'd jumped at the opportunity to be just Ben, not a firefighter, not the man in charge, not the son who'd been forced to accept responsibilities he'd been too young to shoulder. For those few hours, he'd chosen to forget why he'd even been at the bar that night, never once believing the decision would come back to bite him in the butt.

He looked at Jana. No easy, welcoming smile curved

her lips today; they were a tight grim line. She didn't resemble the Jana he knew. The navy power suit and crisp white blouse, combined with the sensible all-business hairstyle irked him as much as the accusation in her sharp tone. He preferred the softer Jana, the one that cried his name during the height of pleasure.

She fell back into the desk chair, propped her elbow on the arm and rested her chin in her hand. "What am I supposed to do now?" she murmured, not looking at him.

The way he saw it, she had only one available option. "Reassign the investigation," he told her.

Slowly, she lowered her arm and shot him another heated glance. A deep frown hardened her pretty features. "I don't think so," she snapped at him.

He wasn't the one to blame here, and he didn't appreciate her sniping at him. In two long strides, he crossed the small office, planted his hands on the desk and leaned forward as she'd done earlier.

"You don't have a choice." He kept his voice low so they wouldn't be overheard. "Conflict of interest, Jana. Ring a bell?"

"No." Her frown matched her own low, forceful tone. "This is *my* case. *My* investigation. Got it?"

"You don't have a choice," he said again, only louder.

"I will not have this case reassigned just because we..." Her frown deepened. "Just because we had a one-night stand." She finished the sentence in a rush.

His usual stoicism slipped. Because of her crude assessment of what they'd done? Because she'd dismissed the unique chemistry between them he couldn't possibly ignore? Or because it looked as if his chances of getting laid tonight were circling the drain?

For his own peace of mind, he hoped for the latter. Unfortunately, he suspected the culprit for his annoyance with her stemmed from the former. "We shot past the definition of a one-night stand when you agreed to have dinner with me tonight," he argued.

She narrowed her eyes and let out a hiss of breath as she stood to face him down. "If you think I'm going to jeopardize my career because we had great sex, then think again. It's not going to happen."

He straightened as she circled the desk. "Reassigning a case won't hurt your career, Jana, but continuing under the circumstances could. I was the one in charge out there. I'm the one that sent Fitz into that house. The fact that we're involved will have an effect on your objectivity. You have to see that."

She folded her arms and glared at him. "Involved?" Her caustic little laugh shook loose his carefully controlled temper. "We are *not* involved."

"How do you figure that?" He matched her stance and her glare. "Recap. You ask to buy me a drink. You invite me back to your place. We make love." He leaned toward her and held her narrowed gaze. "Correction. We make love all night long."

She looked away. "That does not mean we're involved."

The sharp edge of anger in her voice dug in and took hold. "You called me," he continued hotly. "You agreed to go out with me tonight. We even played around with phone sex, in case that escaped your memory, too. Starting to sound a little like involvement? You seeing a conflict of interest yet?"

"You're the one who sent me flowers." The delicate pink blush tingeing her cheeks took the punch right out of her argument.

"It was your decision to call." The volume of his voice rose another notch, but he was beyond caring. "If you hadn't wanted to see where this is headed, you wouldn't have bothered to pick up the phone."

She dropped her hands to her side and faced him. Heat and frustration lined her gaze. "Why is this my fault all of a sudden?"

He moved back to the desk and perched on the edge to gain some distance, and he hoped, perspective. "I'm just telling you that you can't be the one to investigate the incident." He struggled for an infusion of calm, rational thought. It didn't happen. "I'm not blaming you."

"It sure sounds as if you are," she argued. "And I really don't care what you think. I'm not handing my investigation off to someone else because my being here makes you uncomfortable."

He let out a sigh, but his temper failed to ebb. *Determined* didn't begin to describe this side of her he'd just been introduced to, and he didn't like what he was seeing. *Bullheaded, impossibly stubborn, unable to see reason* were more accurate. And, heaven help him, sexy as hell. He wanted her. Now. He wanted all that passion channeled into something a whole lot more satisfying than an argument.

"How is it going to look if you stay on the case?" he countered. "Your objectivity is going to be questioned."

"I'm a professional. I won't let that happen."

Faced with her unwillingness to listen to reason, his last shred of tolerance crashed. Hard. "Dammit, Jana," he thundered, pushing off the desk.

Jana's eyes widened in surprise at his outburst, stopping him cold.

He raked his hand through his hair, then pulled in a deep steadying breath that scarcely calmed him. What the hell was wrong with him? He didn't lose his cool. He never blustered and never shouted, especially at a woman. He was nothing like his old man, but after his outburst, he'd have a rough time defending himself.

Reeling in his temper took supreme effort. Where had the standard cool, detached manner he'd perfected over the years gone? he wondered. Where was the cold-hearted, unemotional bastard now, the one he'd been accused of being on more than one occasion?

He wished he knew.

"I'm sorry about that," he told Jana.

She indicated her acceptance of his apology with a slight nod of her head.

With a calm he had yet to salvage fully, he asked her, "Why can't you see this has disaster written all over it?"

She let out a weighty sigh, then sat on the edge of the guest chair. "It's only a disaster if we keep seeing each other."

She couldn't possibly be serious, could she?

"At least, as long as I'm conducting my investigation," she continued, "our involvement will remain strictly professional."

The firmness in her voice told him she was dead serious, disappointing him. Since leaving her apartment, he'd been hovering near obsession anticipating the next time they'd be together.

He didn't fault her for her dedication to her career. On that level, he did understand her hesitation to hand the case over to another investigator. Obviously, Ben wasn't thinking with the head above his shoulders because he couldn't understand the ease with which she ignored the attraction and chemistry that sizzled between them. Was the woman blind?

He let out a harsh breath. He'd just have to *make* her see the problem. If she refused to reassign the case, then she left him with no choice but to show her the reality of her flawed reasoning. Stooping to drastic measures in order to clear her cloudy vision suddenly made perfect sense to him.

He snagged her hand and urged her out of the chair and into his arms. "It'll never work," he said with renewed confidence.

Wariness filled her gaze, but she didn't resist him. "Yes, it will." She didn't sound convinced.

Good.

Her strictly professional argument crumbled like dust the instant he dipped his head to nuzzle her ear. She trembled, then gave a soft, gentle moan and a need-drenched whisper of his name.

"Shhh." He took her earlobe lightly between his teeth. "There's nothing professional about the way you make me feel, Jana," he whispered. "Or the way your body responds to mine."

Before she had the chance to argue with him, he slid his mouth over hers and kissed her deeply. She issued another sexy little moan and wrapped her arms around his neck. Victory never tasted sweeter.

Her slender body brushed enticingly against his, sending a flaming ball of heat south, hardening him, filling him with gut-clawing need. He kissed his way back to nuzzle the side of her neck, breathing in more of her intoxicating, exotic scent. "Definitely not professional," he whispered against her satiny skin.

She clung to him and tipped her head to the side. He pressed his tongue against the rapid pulse beating at the side of her throat.

She let out a sigh. "Couldn't this be construed as sexual harassment?"

He pulled back, encouraged by the desire darkening the color of her eyes. "Nope," he answered with a slow shake of his head. "You kissed me back."

He sensed her reluctance as she moved out of his embrace. He wanted her close. He wanted her naked and beneath him, crying his name as wave after wave of passion rocked her world. Something he planned to remedy as soon as humanly possible.

"I admit it. Working together won't be easy," she said. "But you have to understand that my job comes first."

Jana had a knack for saying the magic words, and just his luck, she reached past his arguments and grabbed hold of his professional jugular. The job *always* came first, no matter what. He had to respect that—to a point.

"I won't reassign the case," she continued. "Business and pleasure can't mix, that much is obvious. Once I file my report, we'll see what happens. Agreed?"

"Agreed," he said, not exactly truthful. He agreed that business and pleasure shouldn't co-exist, especially in their case, but no way was he going to wait until she concluded the investigation to have her in his bed. In fact, he arrogantly believed once he proved his point— that business was nowhere near as gratifying as their mutual pleasure—she'd wing the case file off to another investigator *pronto*.

His smile widened into a grin at the thought of all the tantalizing possibilities and pleasures ahead. "Yeah," he said, slowly. "We *will* see what happens."

BY THE TIME Jana walked into her apartment at the end of the day, she was physically and emotionally exhausted. She put her briefcase and purse away in the coat closet as she did every night, then marched straight to the bathroom for a hot shower.

She needed to relax, wash away the stress caused by a long, arduous day spent interviewing fire department personnel. Toss in the tension making her skin feel so tight and her body incredibly achy for a certain man's touch, and she was ready to shriek in frustration. Ben had quashed her professional argument when he'd effortlessly stoked a simmering flame into a two-alarm blaze she'd been unable to douse, all with one little nibble on her ear.

She'd just have to be stronger next time. How to manage that exactly, escaped her.

Thanks to the minor squabble she and Ben had had in the captain's office, the squad knew for certain they were involved. To top it off, as she conducted her interviews, she realized that some of the members had even been at the Ivory Turtle on Friday night.

In the name of self-preservation, she'd opted to skip Ben's interview until tomorrow. Although she hadn't seen much of him for the remainder of the day, thanks to that fantasy-inducing kiss and her body's instant recognition of his, he'd never been far from her thoughts.

She stripped down, folded her clothes and carefully sorted them into the appropriate laundry hampers, then removed her makeup and took down her hair while the water heated. She hadn't actually expected the squad to openly share information with an outsider, and they'd hardly disappointed her. Obtaining specific details had been excruciating. The official reports contained more information than she'd been able to glean from the tight-knit group of Station 43.

"The more tragic the occurrence, the tighter the lips," she muttered to her reflection.

With one exception, she thought, stepping beneath the hot, stinging spray of the shower. Arson Investigator Drew Perry, whom she recognized from that night at the Ivory Turtle. She'd been surprised to learn that he was actually Ben's youngest brother. She'd even discovered another brother, Cale, worked out of Trinity Station as a paramedic, although he hadn't been on duty today, or at the scene that had taken the life of FF2 Ivan Fitzpatrick.

According to Drew's report, two firefighters had entered the residence to save a young mother and her two small children. The family had been rescued and one firefighter had made it out, but Fitzpatrick had been overcome by smoke. By the time he'd radioed for help, the roof of the structure had collapsed and it'd been too late.

The information Drew gave her hadn't been much more than she'd read herself, or what other members of the squad had told her. However, there'd been one small exception—RIT, the Rapid Intervention Team of the specially trained firefighters sent into buildings to retrieve emergency personnel in trouble, hadn't gone in for Fitzpatrick.

RIT had been summoned, but by the time they'd arrived, scene safety had prevented the team from entering the residence. The prospect of determining why the team hadn't been called sooner filled her with dread. The responsibility fell under the direction of the incident commander—Ben. A fact which lent strength to her argument of keeping their relationship strictly professional for the moment.

She turned her back to the spray, but the steaming water was a useless tool against her apprehension. If she determined Ben was at fault, she seriously doubted their chance of a future relationship.

No. She wouldn't think about that. Her job was to assess and analyze the situation, determine if the cause of the fatality was an accident or human error, then provide the fire department with her recommendations in hopes of avoiding a similar tragedy in the future. Her feelings for Ben could not, *would not*, interfere. She would maintain her objectivity, provided she learned to ignore all those delicious cravings he kept stirring up inside her.

After washing her hair, she left the shower and dried off before slipping into her fluffy chenille robe. She didn't bother to dress since she planned nothing more taxing than a bowl of anything she could heat in the micro. Since she wouldn't be seeing Ben tonight, her evening entertainment would consist of the nightly news and whatever reality show happened to be scheduled, before she slipped into the warmth of her new set of flannel sheets.

Alone, her conscience taunted.

She picked up the remote control from the shelf where she always left it, and surfed to her favorite news channel. The soothing tones of the anchor's voice filled her small apartment with talk of global unrest and the state of the economy. She considered slipping a romantic comedy into the DVD player, but the doom and gloom suited her mood at the moment.

She wandered into the compact kitchen for something cold to drink. Tugging open the fridge, she leaned against the door and peered inside until she decided on a glass of juice.

Tomorrow didn't look as if it'd be any less stressful, either, she thought with a weighty sigh. Ben would be visiting the incident scene with her, which translated to her spending a good portion of her day in his company. Alone. An unnerving, yet exciting, prospect.

As she reached into the overhead cabinet for a can of soup, the doorbell chimed. Her fingers tightened around the can. She might live in a secure building, but that didn't necessarily mean a nonresident couldn't be granted access. Something a man as determined as Ben could easily manage.

Tiny pinpricks of excitement coated her skin. She was being ridiculous. It was *not* him. They'd agreed not to see each other. He didn't strike her as the kind of man to go back on his word.

The bell chimed a second time. With a sigh, she set the soup on the counter and glanced at the wall clock above the small dining table in the eating area. A few minutes before seven. Chloe and Lauren rarely popped over without calling first. Neither would Jana's sisters, and especially not her mother. Her father's secretary would've called to schedule an actual appointment.

She tightened the sash of her robe on the way to the door. She was definitely being ridiculous, she thought. The downstairs neighbor probably wanted to borrow her blender again.

A quick look through the peephole sent her stomach careening down to her toes like a roller coaster.

She muttered a soft curse and yanked opened the door. The emotional roller coaster shot off to the left, leaving her momentarily stunned by the all-too-delicious sight of him. He'd changed out of his uniform into a pair of dark denim jeans and a white oxford shirt with pencil-thin, pale blue stripes she'd wager matched his eyes. His slightly damp thick, black hair curled at the ends. The half smile turning up one corner of his mouth made him look scrumptious, and impossible for her to resist.

She planted one hand on the doorjamb and the other on the door in an intentionally unwelcome gesture and frowned. "Why are you here?"

The scoundrel's sexy smile widened. "We had a date, remember?"

"We agreed not to see each other," she reminded him.

"There's no harm in having dinner together." He held a large brown paper bag in one arm.

Her fingers tightened around the door frame. "We shouldn't." Not *we can't*, or *no, I won't. Shouldn't.* Total wimp response.

He inched closer, and she breathed in his rich scent. Male, a little spicy and a whole lot…Italian? Her tummy grumbled. The cad was bribing her with food.

"We really shouldn't." Definitely a lack of the appropriate level of conviction to send him on his way.

"What if we both promise not to mention the investigation?"

She bit her bottom lip, completely tempted.

"You need to eat," he coaxed, using that deep, seductive tone she adored. And so very close to the one he used when they made love. "There's nothing wrong with two people sharing a meal."

Or a bed?

She didn't say it, but the unspoken words still hung between them, part threat, part promise.

Well, she *was* hungry. On both counts. Minestrone and grape juice hardly qualified as a decent meal. Snuggling with Ben between the sheets scarcely met the definition of professionalism, but he *had* brought food. Italian food, too. Her absolute favorite. A faltering willpower overruled any thoughts of objectivity.

Quick! Shut the door and order a pizza before it's too late!

She shoved her better judgment out the door and hoped it tumbled down the stairs. "*Just* dinner." She stepped back to motion him inside her apartment. "One word about the investigation," she warned, "and you're outta here."

One word about pleasure, and she'd be out of her mind with desire. An acute condition with no cure.

Well, there was one cure. A pleasurable, addicting cure, twice as dangerous as the ailment.

8

BEN FOLLOWED Jana into the small efficiency kitchen, his gaze traveling from the curve of her waist to the enticing sway of her bottom beneath a thick, fuzzy robe. He had no idea what, if anything, she wore beneath, but he intended to enjoy fully every nanosecond of discovery. Later.

"I wasn't sure I could convince you." He set the bag on the small counter space. "I'd hoped food in hand would do the trick."

"Smart man." Her eyes brightened as she eagerly peered into the bag and inhaled deeply. "Oh God, that smells incredible."

Incredible summed up the view of her breasts as she leaned forward to breathe in the tempting aroma of stuffed shells with marinara sauce and fresh-baked crusty bread tucked inside the bag. A bottle of spumante and an antipasto salad completed the meal he'd ordered earlier in the day.

He was a man with a plan, armed with ammunition. After a night of intense seduction to show her what she'd be missing if she didn't reassign the investigation, he was confident OSHA would be sending a new rep to the firehouse in her place—provided Ben kept his control tightly in check. Considering how much he wanted her already, his plan had every chance of backfiring.

The warmth of her smile made him feel just a tad guilty. Based on her reaction to their lovemaking Friday night, she just might do him physical harm if he left her in a state of physical arousal.

"You," she said, her voice infused with laughter, "do not play fair."

The urge to pull her into his arms and kiss her stupid shook him. With monumental effort, he tamped the need—for the time being. "What's so unfair about dinner?" To keep from hauling her against him, he transferred the food and wine from the bag to the counter.

She went to the cabinet for dishes. "Care to explain this uncanny knack you seem to have for knowing what I need, exactly when I need it?"

Ideas about what she needed, and just how he hoped to deliver, tempted him beyond his wildest fantasies. Not yet, he reminded himself. In about forty minutes sounded good to him. Provided he lasted that long. "You needed Italian food?"

She handed him a pair of salad tongs and two bowls. "Not exactly, but the wine is welcome."

He concentrated on tossing the salad. "Rough day?" he asked, but he already knew the answer. From his conversations throughout the day with the crew, they hadn't exactly been cooperative. Ben's influence over his men was limited, and while he understood OSHA needing to start their investigation quickly, most OSHA reps failed to recognize how raw the emotions were or how deep the unhealed wounds still ran. It'd take time for the guys to be able to talk openly about the incident. Unloading during the stress debriefings the department scheduled did help them learn to cope, but those meetings were a safe haven, a place for the guys to vent and come to terms with the horrors they experienced on the job. They saw OSHA as the enemy, where a misspoken word could easily be misinterpreted. Accepting the loss of a fallen member of the team was in a different league from opening up to someone looking to assign blame.

She let out a sigh. "Let's just say I could stand to relax a little. Changing the subject would help, too."

A glass or two of wine ran a sorry second to the relaxation method he preferred. He let out a rough sigh, reining in the lascivious images.

With her arms laden with plates, silverware and linen napkins with matching place mats, she handed him a can of soup on her way to the table.

"What do you want me to do with this?" he asked, holding up the can.

"Right there." She pointed to the overhead cabinet in front of him.

He opened the cabinet and stared. Canned fruit and vegetables lined the bottom shelf, spaced evenly apart, fruit on the right, veggies on the left. Above on the second shelf sat perfectly arranged and stacked rows of soup cans. The top shelf housed all the odd-shaped cans, placed in order by size. He turned his attention to Jana. She set the table, carefully adjusting the silverware a precise distance from the plates, making sure the bottom edges were in exact alignment.

She must've sensed his gaze, because she glanced

over her shoulder. She frowned, her expression quizzical. "Just put it on top of the other can of minestrone," she said. "Between the hearty chicken and New England clam chowder."

He placed the can where she'd instructed, then closed the cabinet door. "You're anal," he said, unable to keep the amusement from of his voice.

She rolled her eyes and went back to straightening the already perfectly set table. "Organization is not a crime."

"You alphabetize your canned goods." His laughter erupted. "That's not organized, babe, that's obsessive."

She shrugged her slim shoulders, but still wouldn't look at him. A tentative smile curved the mouth he couldn't wait to taste again. The slight blush coloring her cheeks made her look so adorable he doubted his ability to remain in hands-off mode for much longer.

While she finished with the table, he popped open the spumante. "Glasses?" he asked.

She pulled out a chair and sat, then unfolded a napkin to set in her lap. "Top cabinet, left of the sink."

Unlike his own mismatched dishes of unknown origin, plastic convenience-store tumblers and some old coffee mugs, her dishes and glassware were perfectly coordinated and impeccably stored by size and function, in evenly spaced rows and columns. He'd never dreamed a die-hard perfectionist lurked inside such a wild, uninhibited lover.

Almost uninhibited, he amended. While she wasn't shy with her body, she hadn't exactly told him what she liked, either. Although he thought her cries of *Yes. Oh,*

Ben. Yes, had been highly erotic, he would've welcomed a bit more communication on her part.

He snagged the sack with condiments, then carried it to the table with the wine and long-stemmed glassware. A horrified expression lined her face when he dumped the contents of the white bag on the wood surface. "Something the matter?"

She plucked a square, foil packet of Parmesan cheese from the table and held it between her fingers. She looked as if he'd tossed an offensive pair of sweaty gym socks left too long in a locker in front of her. "You don't really eat this stuff, do you?"

He poured the wine and shrugged. "You have issues with cheese?"

She scooped up the other packets and carried them to the garbage can tucked beneath the sink. "Cheese, no. Cardboard, absolutely."

She opened the fridge and returned with a plastic container of hand-grated Parmesan. "Much better," she murmured, sprinkling a liberal amount over the small portion she'd served herself. She took a bite, then moaned with delight.

She looked at him and murmured something he didn't catch. He was still processing that husky moan and savoring a new fantasy. One that had him clearing the table with a sweep of his arm, tugging the knot of her robe loose and seeing for himself exactly what she wore underneath. Nothing, he hoped.

"Ben?"

Her laughter nudged him back to reality. The amusement in her eyes had him wondering if she knew exactly where his mind had wandered.

"Did you say something?" he asked.

"This was really very nice of you." A grateful smile curved her lips, pale and unlipsticked and quite inviting. "Thank you."

"I aim to please."

Heat flared in her eyes. She dipped her head to concentrate on her plate. "I didn't know you had brothers," she said, her tone brisk. "I met one of them today."

He reluctantly tucked the fantasy away. "If you're at the firehouse tomorrow, you'll probably meet Cale."

If? Jana mused. She should just live for the moment and stop worrying that Ben had some ulterior motive for showing up at her apartment. Well, one reason was obvious, she amended. The desire she detected gave him away. Unfortunately, her suspicions were operating on high, thanks to their argument that morning.

"So, do you still boss them around?" she asked, deciding to ignore that curious "if." It could be a few days, or possibly a couple of weeks before she wrapped up her investigation, so she might as well take what little time together they did have and enjoy the moment.

He frowned as he tore off a chunk of the warm bread. "Why? What did Drew tell you?"

"Nothing." She laughed despite the wariness she couldn't completely ignore. "I have personal experience with first-born siblings, that's all."

"Where do you fall on the family food chain?"

"Bottom feeder. All girls."

"I'm familiar with the type."

"Oh really?" she asked. "And what type is that?"

He slathered butter over the bread. "Either you did everything you could to stand out and be noticed, or you were the good little girl." He set the knife on the edge of his plate. "Considering your...organizational skills," he said with a quick grin, "I'd say good girl, but you've got a temper, so that pretty much blows my theory."

Not exactly the epitome of calm himself, he had no business chucking bricks at her behavior. She'd been surprised by his outburst, but hardly alarmed. He simply didn't come off as one of those jerky types that bullied women to feel better about themselves. Ben had way too much confidence. He hardly needed to feed a lacking self-esteem.

"I wasn't rebellious," she told him, "but I did have a tendency toward stubbornness that would get me into trouble."

He lifted his eyebrows. "A hellion, huh?"

"Hardly," she scoffed, before taking a bite of her salad. "Well, there was the time Caroline dared me to sneak out to a party with her. That one cost me a few stitches."

He looked at her quizzically for a moment, and she just knew he was replaying Friday night. Suddenly, he flashed her that rascal's grin she'd never be able to resist.

"Ahh," he said, slowly. "That's where you got the scar on your—"

She cleared her throat. "That would be the one," she said quickly. Not one of her proudest moments. The two-inch scar on her backside served as a constant reminder. "One reason why you'll never see me in a thong swimsuit."

The color of his eyes darkened. "Now that *is* a crime."

Her pulse picked up speed. "I must've been around six or seven when I refused to eat vegetables," she said, forcing herself to concentrate on their conversation rather than the awareness prickling her skin.

"Most kids decide they don't like vegetables at some point." He shrugged his wide shoulders. "I still won't eat lima beans or peas."

"I bet you didn't raid the freezer and the pantry, then hand all the vegetables out to the neighbors."

He chuckled, a deep, low rumbling sound that warmed her. "You couldn't have just thrown them away?"

"Heavens, no," she said with mock indignation. "I would've gotten in serious trouble for wasting food. There were children starving in third-world countries, you know."

"Tell me more," he coaxed, then dug into his salad.

She loved his smile, and the way his eyes crinkled slightly at the corners when he laughed. While she'd been distracted with all that incredible afterglow stuff, he'd snuck past one-night stand status straight into involvement. With every second she spent with him, her emotional apprehension grew. Falling for Ben would be so easy. Too easy. After only three days she already suspected her heart might be at risk, which meant she could end up getting hurt when their affair eventually ended.

By the time they moved into the living room with re-filled glasses of wine nearly an hour later, she'd shared with him most of her embarrassing moments from childhood. She gave him points for being a good listener, a component the male psyche generally lacked.

"What about you?" She pulled two coasters from the holder and set them on the coffee table. "I've been talking about myself all night. Any moments of teenage rebellion, or were you too busy bossing around your brothers?"

His smile faded somewhat, his expression shifting to something she thought could be longing. Her curiosity spiked.

"There's not much to tell."

Beside her on the sofa, he sat close enough for the musky tang of his aftershave to tease her senses. His thigh brushed hers, sending sparks traveling over her skin to gather and sizzle in her breasts. Her nipples tightened. "Try me."

Do me! A much more honest statement. A tempting one, too.

He stretched his right arm over the back of the sofa behind her. She suppressed the desire to rest her head against his shoulder. Oh, she could get used to this involvement stuff.

His fingers teased the ends of her hair. "Not much to tell." He took a deep drink from his wineglass. "Normal kid stuff."

She wasn't buying it, but she sensed his unwillingness to discuss his childhood and attempted a more subtle approach. "You're very different from your brother."

"Drew's the youngest." The return of his smile failed to chase away the shadows clouding his gaze. "It's a known fact the youngest is always the brattiest."

Her tactic failed.

Maybe he didn't feel comfortable enough with her yet. No, she didn't buy that one, either. She had her own set of facts to prove otherwise. His easy smiles. The complete and open way he'd loved her. The way he looked at her, as if he were dying of thirst and she held the map to the closest well of cool water. Maybe he had some sort of emotional baggage. That was something she could relate to since she had a trunk or two of her own. Namely her parents, her father in particular. The past shaped a person, and considering the growing respect she had for Ben, she decided whatever had molded him couldn't have been all that bad.

He leaned forward to set the glass on the coaster. "I've given some thought to our situation," he said, changing the subject.

"And?" she asked cautiously. She'd meant what she'd told him. One word about her investigation and he'd have to leave. Just having dinner with him had to contain at least a dozen ethics violations.

"I agree that under the circumstances our involvement is unprofessional," he continued. "Especially when we're on the job. But, a lot of couples work together successfully."

She had trouble digesting his words, since one in particular kept flashing in her brain like a neon billboard. *Couples.* He thought of them as a couple? Not that she minded the reference because it gave her a warm fuzzy feeling that had nothing to do with alcohol. The men in white coats had to be searching for him; she thought the C word was as taboo as the L word in man-speak.

"Excuse me, but wasn't it you that pointed out we had a huge conflict-of-interest problem?"

He nodded as he turned to face her. "Maybe I was too hasty." His hand settled on her knee peeking out from the opening in her robe.

Suddenly, she was very aware that all that separated his hand from the rest of her body was a few yards of chenille. She pulled in a deep breath and let it out slowly. "Go on."

This I've got to hear.

"So long as we keep work out of the bedroom and sex out of the firehouse, why shouldn't we see where this thing between us is headed?"

Leaning. Someone was leaning. Him? Or was that her slowly drifting in his direction? If he'd take his hand off her knee and stop tracing those distracting circles over her skin, she might actually be capable of intelligent conversation.

She forced herself back against the cushion. "I would really like that," she told him honestly. "But, I think you called it right the first time. If my investigation and having an affair with you isn't a conflict of interest, then at the very least it's unethical."

His palm smoothed over her knee and moved upward. Slowly, deliberately, he fanned his fingers, gently

The Harlequin Reader Service® — Here's how it works:

If offer card is missing write to: Harlequin Reader Service, 3010 Walden Ave., P.O. Box 1867, Buffalo NY 14240-1867

NO POSTAGE
NECESSARY
IF MAILED
IN THE
UNITED STATES

BUSINESS REPLY MAIL
FIRST-CLASS MAIL   PERMIT NO. 717-003   BUFFALO, NY

POSTAGE WILL BE PAID BY ADDRESSEE

HARLEQUIN READER SERVICE
3010 WALDEN AVE
PO BOX 1867
BUFFALO NY 14240-9952

easing his hand higher up her thigh. While he'd been busy distracting her with his touch, she realized he'd moved in close enough for her to see the dark rim surrounding his pale-blue irises. And his determination.

"That's too bad." His voice turned low and husky. His hand advanced a few millimeters higher. "That would mean no back rubs."

Oh boy, he absolutely did not play fair. Something in her tummy tugged hard, sending a flow of warmth through her veins to settle between her legs. Her entire body hummed with anticipation.

He moved in and nibbled her bottom lip. "No kisses, either," he whispered, then lured her into a hot, wet, deep kiss.

Under the influence of his seductive spell, she willingly followed him. Her skin prickled. Dampness pooled between her legs. Struggling against the intense, instant craving to mate with him sounded like a dumb idea to her. She wondered if he had an aversion to flannel sheets.

His tongue slid over hers, teasing and retreating then becoming more bold and demanding. She issued a few demands of her own, then slipped her hand behind his neck to sift her fingers through the thick, silky strands of his black-as-midnight hair.

His fingers skimmed lightly through her curls. Forget flannel sheets. The sofa worked for her.

He ended the kiss far too quickly, but she forgot to complain when his lips trailed a path from her jaw to the sensitive spot below her ear. She felt a quick pull at her waist followed by cool air brushing against her heated skin as he parted her robe. With one hand cupping the back of her head, he used his other to run his fingers over her rib cage, then palmed her breast as if testing the weight.

"No touching, either." The words whispered in her ear barely registered through the sensual fog clouding her mind. Concentration was impossible with him scraping his thumb lightly over her nipple and nibbling on her neck.

"Ben," she murmured and closed her eyes. She didn't care if she sounded needy and breathless. She wanted him inside her. Now that she'd had a taste of what they could share, she wanted him in the worst way. The ache ran deep and was too powerful to deny. If he didn't ease the tension, she couldn't be held responsible for her actions.

"No climaxes, Jana." His hand slid slowly down her stomach. Lower. Lower, until he combed his fingers through her curls. She parted her legs, anticipating his intimate touch.

He slid over her slick folds to the core of her to caress her gently. Dipping deep inside, he then retreated to cover her with moisture. His thumb applied the perfect blend of pressure to her most sensitive place.

Oh yes. She definitely could get used to this.

"Do you really want to go without now that you know how incredible it feels when you fall apart? When we come apart? Together?"

She bit her lip before she whimpered like a pup begging for a handout. The pressure magnified, climbing higher and higher with each stroke of his hand until her body trembled, dangling on the precipice of release. She clung to his shoulder with one hand, while the other gripped the arm of the sofa so hard her hand ached.

"Will you come now, Jana?"

She arched against his hand.

"Come for me now," he coaxed her, then clamped his mouth down hard over hers.

The sensations ruling her body took over and consumed her. The sweep and demand of his tongue mimicked the thrust of his hand until she couldn't breathe. The fierce strength of her release sent her crashing over the edge where the world exploded. He swallowed her fierce cries as she instinctively sought more of the delicious, liquid heat filling every inch of her by lifting her hips.

She had no idea how much time passed as he gently eased her back to earth. Reality held a hint of musk in the air and an insistent beeping she didn't recognize, followed by the warmth of chenille being tucked around her. She opened her eyes when she heard him sigh.

"But, you're probably right." He stood slowly, then pulled his beeper from his belt. "It would be unethical for us to do any of that while we're working together."

She watched in horror as he reclipped the beeper and slipped a set of keys from his pocket. He couldn't be leaving. Sure, he'd definitely satisfied her, but...but she wanted more. She wanted *all* of him. "Where do you think you're going?"

A sexy little half smile kicked up one corner of his mouth. "Work."

A sweeping glance down his body offered visual proof of his arousal. Desire shone bright in his eyes, but still...but he was...*leaving?* He couldn't do this to her. Not again.

She stood and jerked hard on the sash of her robe, knotting it tight around her. She ached for more of his touch.

"Why are you doing this?" she demanded. "I thought you were off duty?" How could he leave her feeling so...so incomplete, still craving him? He'd warmed her up to simmering and now he planned to walk away before they could reach a full boil—together?

He shrugged. "I'm needed."

The man deserved to be shot for that remark. Didn't he realize she needed him to finish what he'd started?

His smile deepened. "Besides, you wouldn't want to jeopardize your investigation now, would you?"

She fisted her hands at her sides so she wouldn't wing the closest object at his arrogant head.

He walked to the door and opened it. "Think about what you'll be missing until you close the case."

Before she could summon a scathing reply, or chuck a coaster at his head, he slipped out the door. Damn him. She knew exactly what she'd be missing. Hot. Wet. Thoroughly exciting, all-night-long sex. With a man playing the oldest game around until she gave him what he wanted—her off the case.

She hurled a few obscenities she hoped would have

his ears ringing as she headed toward the shower. Once the water heated, she stepped beneath the spray, partially comforted by the thought of Ben in such an obvious state of arousal and his inability to do a single thing about it.

Despite her own frustration, she managed a giggle, and *almost* felt sorry for him.

9

JANA KNOCKED LIGHTLY on the open door to her boss's office. "Got a minute?"

Gwen Reedly glanced up from the thick binder filled with computer printouts she'd been reviewing and smiled warmly as she waved Jana into the office. "I'm glad you stopped by. I was going to ask you to come by because I need to speak with you anyway." She picked up the phone and dialed. "Have a seat and give me two minutes."

Jana nodded, trying not to feel paranoid. Had Gwen heard about her and Ben already?

She let out a quiet sigh and sat in the gray fabric office chair, shifting her attention to the skyline of high-rise buildings as Gwen made her phone call. Although she'd been arguing with Ben that she would not, under any circumstances, reassign the investigation, this morning she'd reluctantly come to the conclusion that she had no choice but to make Gwen aware a conflict of interest existed.

The decision hadn't been an easy one, and Jana dreaded having to admit that something personal could interfere with her objectivity on the job. After last night's deliciously naughty, albeit preempted rendezvous, her ability to separate her growing feelings for the man who turned her inside out with little effort from her objectivity about the firefighter she'd been sent to investigate was questionable.

But more importantly, her stubborn refusal even to consider reassigning the case was far too reminiscent of her father. And since Jana refused to follow in her father's footsteps, she'd decided to inform Gwen of the problem and see about being removed from the investigation.

Kyle Linney had put his career before anything else in his life. Without a second thought he'd sacrificed what should've mattered most—his wife and daughters. Granted, her father was an enormously successful documentary director, but not a single one of the awards displayed in his offices would offer him companionship in his old age. Not that she honestly believed she and Ben were going to spend the rest of their lives together, but she could easily be sacrificing her hard-earned career, and maybe even her financial independence, if she refused to divulge the truth.

Gwen hung up the phone and turned to Jana. "I realize this is short notice, but please tell me you don't have plans for the weekend." She slipped a slim gold hoop earring back in place.

"No," Jana told her. "Nothing."

Jana greatly admired Gwen. She hadn't believed her good fortune when she'd learned her promotion would include a transfer to Gwen Reedly's team in the fire-investigation division. Following her investigation of a high-rise fire two decades ago, Gwen had been responsible for many of the changes in the way fire departments handled emergency rescue operations in Los Angeles County. The blaze had gutted a dozen floors and taken the lives of eight firefighters. The woman was practically a legend in public administration, but she'd also acquired a reputation as a tough-as-railroad-spikes businesswoman.

That knowledge alone made Jana's task that much more unsettling. How did she explain to a woman who'd risen to Gwen's level that she couldn't keep her panties on whenever she came within ten feet of Ben?

"I apologize for the short notice." Gwen settled back in the faux leather executive chair. "We need a warm body from this division to attend a training meeting in Carmel. It's a full schedule on Friday, then Saturday until noon. Interested?"

"In spending a weekend in Carmel?" Relieved, Jana smiled. "I wouldn't consider it an inconvenience."

"Good. See Heather on the way out and she'll set everything up for you. Unless you're psychic, I'm guessing you came in to see me about something. What's up?"

Jana settled her elbows on the arms of the chair, praying for the strength to survive whatever came next. "You need to be aware of a potential situation."

Gwen removed her tortoise-shell glasses and set them on the desk. "Are you having trouble getting the squad to cooperate?"

Jana shook her head. "No," she said. "Actually, they haven't been too bad, considering. I have a concern about a conflict of interest."

Gwen leaned forward and clasped her hands together. "What kind of conflict?"

"I'm involved with one of the firefighters at Trinity Station."

The warmth faded from Gwen's expression, replaced by concern. "I see," the older woman said carefully. "May I ask exactly how involved you are with him?"

Jana's apprehension tripled. She had hoped to avoid this part of the conversation. The embarrassing part. "Intimately involved."

Once again, she had to face the ramifications of her stubborn nature. If she hadn't taken that stupid dare, she never would've had to admit something so personal, not only to her boss, but to the woman she admired. Would she ever learn? The next time someone dared her to do anything, she was walking away, if only to save her from herself.

"You should've said something when I assigned you this case," Gwen said with the barest hint of censure. "I could've given it to Davis or Walker."

She pulled in a steadying breath. "I'm not proud of the fact," Jana said, "but I didn't know him when you gave me the case."

The sound of male voices drifted through the open door. Gwen stood and crossed the office, quietly closing the door. To read her the riot act or ensure their conversation remained private? Jana hoped for the latter. This was not the kind of gossip, nor the impression, she wanted spread among her co-workers.

Gwen returned, taking the vacant chair next to Jana. "Explain this to me."

Jana let out a sigh, semi-relieved. "I met him Friday night," she said. "I honestly didn't think I'd ever see him again, but..." *But he has this way of making me insane with need. Jeez, I just can't keep my hands off him.*

"But," Gwen finished for her, "you clicked."

"And then some," Jana muttered.

Gwen didn't appear angry, but her dark-brown eyes widened a fraction. Definitely not encouraging.

"We didn't talk about our jobs," Jana continued, "so I was clueless about him being a firefighter. I showed up at Station 43 yesterday morning and found out he's not only a lieutenant with the department, but the scene commander in charge at the time of the incident."

Gwen's displeasure became obvious. "You know, Jana," she said. "I've heard a lot and seen more, but *this* is the first time an investigation's been compromised because my lead investigator is sleeping with a lieutenant in the fire department."

Jana had her own list of firsts she had no intention of sharing with her boss. "How should I handle the situation?"

"Well," Gwen said, "we definitely have a problem, especially if you determine fault lies with this guy. No one is available to take over for you, either. Davis and Walker both have fresh assignments. I haven't even started finding people for your team, so that eliminates the possibility of allowing you to distance yourself from the on-site investigation."

Gwen was thoughtful for a moment, then shook her head as if discarding an idea. "I've got three supervisors on the Terminal Island industrial complex case, and can't spare anyone there since we're still looking at around three to four weeks to wrap up."

"The nature of the Station 43 incident alone means we can't postpone it," Jana reminded Gwen. "I've already started conducting formal interviews and there are a few things I'd like to reexamine in a more relaxed atmosphere, if I can. I just need to know how you want me to handle it, under the circumstances."

"Look, Jana, I trust your judgment or I wouldn't have given you such a tough assignment in the first place. I should pull you off the case, but I have no one else to fill in for you."

Gwen did not look pleased, but at least she hadn't said she should send Jana packing. For now, at least, her job was safe.

The older woman stood and returned to her desk. "You've made me aware of the problem, and I appreciate it. I'll personally conduct the follow-up of your findings on any non-compliance matters. To cover ourselves, I am going to have to place a call to the captain and let him know what's going on."

Jana stifled a groan. If the captain was like any other members of Trinity Station, he probably already knew his lieutenant and the supervising OSHA rep were tangling the sheets together. She didn't relish having his suspicions confirmed or her credibility questioned, but she couldn't ignore that what she felt for Ben might be more than a garden variety one-night stand.

"In the meantime," Gwen said, picking up the glasses she'd discarded earlier, "continue with the case. If you run into trouble, I'll see what we can do."

Jana stood, not exactly relieved, but she certainly felt better since she wasn't hiding anything from her boss. "Thank you, Gwen," she said. "I'm really sorry about this."

"Jana?" Gwen called, stopping Jana before she reached the door. "One question. What are you going to do if your findings indicate human error and the lieutenant is the one responsible?"

She'd been dreading the prospect herself. "The only thing I can do," she told Gwen. "File my report and hope for the best."

BY THE TIME Ben arrived at the incident scene, Jana was already waiting for him, parked amid a sea of pickup trucks and stake-bed vehicles weighed down with building materials. He pulled the red state-issued sedan behind her car and cut the engine.

With the window rolled down, he rested his arm on the door and watched her leave her sporty white coupe. Her hips swayed gently as she walked toward him, a clipboard tucked beneath her arm. The black slacks she wore, along with low-heeled, sensible shoes, robbed him of the enticing view of her shapely legs he'd been anticipating. A short red blazer and black blouse downplayed the curves he couldn't wait to touch.

Not only had his plan last night backfired on him— big time—but he had an acute case of lust-induced sleep deprivation which had put him in a sour mood. The constant clawing need in his gut hadn't helped, either, something he blamed on Jana. His minor obsession with her had tripled. She almost constantly occupied his mind, haunting what little sleep he'd managed and filling his head with ridiculous musings about her being a part of his life.

For as long as their involvement might last, he amended. Or at least until she started nagging him about the dangers of his job. Like the others before her, she'd eventually wake up to the fact that nothing would ever change his mind about being a firefighter and she'd be out the door.

The thought did little to improve his mood.

Ben exited the car and slammed the door shut. "Still on the case, I see."

She stopped short at his brusque tone, but he didn't much give a rip at the moment. He wanted her off the investigation. Given his current state of frustration, getting laid had a whole lot to do with it, that he wouldn't deny. But, he wasn't exactly thrilled about her poking inside a gaping wound, either.

Using her hand to shield her eyes from the sun, she looked up at him. A saccharine smile suddenly curved her lips.

She took a few steps toward his car and leaned against the front end, casually crossing her ankles. "You were expecting someone else?" she sassed.

He expelled a harsh breath. "It would've been nice."

"You're a ray of sunshine this morning." Her smile deepened and one of her eyebrows winged upward. Steely determination gave her green eyes a hard cast. "Feeling a bit on edge, are you?"

She sounded way too chipper. And seductive. He'd have to be deaf to ignore the silky quality of her voice.

His annoyance spiked and put him in motion. He circled the car and moved in close.

The flare of desire in her eyes and her sharp intake of breath had the same effect on him as if she'd brushed her fingers over the fly of his trousers. Her hand landed on his chest, but she didn't attempt to push him away. Instead, she spread her fingers over his heart. Damn if he didn't feel her touch clear to his cold, dark soul.

"You wouldn't be in such a pissy mood if you'd stuck around last night," she hissed.

The reminder had his body instantly flexing, giving him something else to concentrate on other than the uncomfortable emotions suddenly crowding him. She had no idea what it had cost him to walk away from her, what it had cost him to bring her pleasure and ignore his own needs. Hours of sleep and an edginess he couldn't afford to suffer while on the job. "I would've stayed if this damned investigation wasn't so important to you."

She pushed him away this time, then scooted off to the side a few feet. "I have a job to do, Ben."

He resented her determination. He despised the fact he couldn't hold her whenever he wanted to because of her refusal to dump the case. "Let someone else do it."

She let out a sigh, then shook her head. "I can't."

"Why the hell won't you let it go?" he growled, taking his frustration out on her.

She shifted the clipboard and held it in front of her. "Maybe I should ask you the same question," she said, a hardness in her voice that equaled the glare she fired his way. "Is there something you don't want me to know?"

Plenty. He'd been the one in charge that day. Fitz had died on his watch because he should've known better than to send him in on a two-in/two-out with a relative greenhorn, who was unaware of Fitz's willingness to risk his hide for a save. Ben had made a bad call and he didn't want her reminding him.

"Answer me, Jana," he demanded, purposely ignoring her question.

The chilled ocean breeze caught a stray wisp of her hair and blew it across her face. She impatiently pushed it back in place. "I tried. That should make you happy."

He crossed his arms over his chest. "You're still here."

Her lips tightened into a thin line and her eyes glittered with temper. The clipboard went sailing through the open window of the department sedan.

"Only because there isn't anyone to cover for me," she said, keeping her voice low as she advanced on him. "What you don't know is that I was very recently promoted to the fire investigation division. This case you're so anxious for me to dump is my first solo assignment. But I went in and told my *new* boss that I had a conflict of interest because I'm sleeping with the man in charge of the incident I'm investigating."

"Aw, hell," he muttered. Guilt rode him hard. "Why didn't you tell me this yesterday? Or last night?" He still didn't like her snooping around, but he liked to think he wouldn't have given her such a hard time if she'd been up-front with him. But he honestly didn't know if it would've made a difference. No other woman had ever twisted him up in so many knots he could barely breathe. Jana managed that and more with something as simple as a glance in his direction or the sound of her voice.

"It's bad enough the men know we're seeing each other. I don't want to even think about how that affects my credibility with them. But how much respect do you really think they'd show me if they found out I was new to FID? Not much, I'll bet." She folded her arms in front of her. "Forget the impression I might have given my boss about me not being capable of handling a tough case because of what's going on between us, but by now, your captain is probably fully aware of the situation."

He swore. Not because Rick would learn about his relationship with Jana, but because for the first time, he saw clearly the problems his determination to lure her back into bed had caused her. "I am sorry. I didn't mean—"

"I don't want your damned apology," she snapped at him. "God, you are so arrogant. You really think I'd put my career on the line for you?"

"That's not what—"

"I realized I had no choice. This is all about ethics. *My* personal ethical boundaries, in particular. I could've lied about us, but when I make my decision, I don't want someone questioning it because of our involvement. I refuse to jeopardize my integrity because of my feelings for you."

She spun around and stormed off toward her car. He

caught up with her before she could yank open the door and escape.

"I am sorry, Jana," he said again.

She crossed her arms and refused to look at him. He lifted his hands to settle them on her shoulders, but stuffed them in the front pockets of his trousers instead.

"I promise I'll respect your decision and keep my distance until you finish the inspection." Because, he realized, he cared about her, too.

She turned to face him. "No pressure?"

"No pressure," he promised. He'd keep his word, even if it killed him.

10

THE OVERCAST SKY shielded the warmth of the early autumn sun and stirred up a cool breeze. The gloom suited Jana's mood, although her earlier irritation had eased somewhat since her outburst. The sting of frustration still plagued her, though, despite Ben's promise of no more pressure. Whether he understood she was talking about both the investigation and their relationship, she wasn't certain, but she had no desire to resurrect the subject again. If things went smoothly, her investigation could be wrapped up in another day or two. Provided they both survived the outcome, they'd be free to explore whatever was happening between them.

Walking alongside Ben toward the base of the foothills to survey the scene, Jana shivered. Her lightweight red blazer offered little warmth. Ben obviously felt the change in temperature, as well, because he tucked his hands into the pockets of the twill bomber-style jacket that matched his dark blue uniform trousers.

His expression turned grim the closer they came to the damage, reminding her of the loss he and the others had suffered. Returning to the scene had to be difficult for him, but she had to keep her concern for his feelings to a minimum. Forcing herself to concentrate on the incident commander who'd been in charge and not on the man who made her pulse race would not be easy.

Carpenters, landscapers and other building professionals littered the area, filling the air with shouted conversations, the pounding of hammers and the drone of power tools. Remnants of the acrid scent of the burn mingled with the smell of freshly cut wood and newly tilled earth in a morbid amalgamation of death and rebirth. A little farther up the hillside on the opposite side of the street, she spied a woman in a dark suit she guessed to be an insurance adjuster. The woman was speaking to a middle-aged couple, assessing the relatively minor repairs needed to the exterior of the residence.

Ben came to a halt midway up the hill and together they stood quietly surveying the area. Although Jana had apologized to him for losing her cool, she still sensed an awkwardness developing between them, in part, she suspected, from the strain of having to revisit the horrible events that had taken place. "Walk me through what happened that morning."

"The initial alarm sounded around eight-thirty," he said. "We were the first squad to respond to the initial 911 call. As soon as we arrived on scene, I assessed the situation and radioed for assistance."

Jana smoothed her hand over the wrinkled pages of the incident report still fastened to the clipboard she'd chucked during her earlier snit. "Within thirty minutes of the first alarm, three more alarms had been struck. Is that right?"

"We had a lot working against us, and weren't capable of handling it alone," he said. "An unusually hot summer and a lengthy heat wave had pretty much dried out the area. Add in mild, but steady, wind coming off the Pacific, air temperature approaching eighty degrees that morning, and you've got a fast-spreading fire."

He hadn't seemed defensive, but the tensing of his shoulders indicated otherwise. After her reaction to his questioning her judgment, she didn't fault him now that his own had come under fire.

"Most of these were older homes." He indicated the still-intact two-story brick structure across the street where she'd spotted the claims adjuster. "The building code for wood-shingle roofs didn't apply when they were constructed. The structures we did save, or that have minimal damage," he continued, "were either newly built or the owners had replaced the old wood shingles with tile."

The building codes had been changed several years ago for all new construction following a devastating fire in the Oakland area that had claimed numerous homes and several lives. If the homes she now surveyed had been built after the revision of the code, the damage might not have been as horrendous.

"You were in charge of seven engine crews, two ladder crews and one rescue, is that correct?"

"We had a total of fifty-seven department personnel on scene," he answered quietly.

And they'd gone home with only fifty-six. He hadn't spoken the words, but the pain that clouded his gaze gave him away.

Jana kept silent. Nothing she could say would alleviate the crew's loss. She suspected Ben, like the rest of the department, carried around a hefty dose of guilt. She tried to understand, but the group harbored something she'd never be able to fully comprehend—the shame of survival. As the man in charge, she supposed Ben's reaction was even more acute than those of his men.

She laid her hand on his forearm. "Are you all right?"

He glanced down at her, and something inside her chest tightened. She'd known revisiting the scene would be difficult for him, but nothing could have prepared her for the emotional toll evident on his handsome face, or her own heart-wrenching reaction.

With one pain-filled glance from Ben, her entire perspective shifted gears. The only thing he could possibly be guilty of was caring about the men under his command.

He moved away. "Let's just get this over with," he said in an abrupt tone.

Frustration returned and played hardball with her professionalism. She no longer wanted to discuss the incident, but rather felt an ache clear to her soul to offer him comfort from the demons that must haunt him.

"Where and how did the fire start?" she asked.

"There." He pointed toward the center of the hillside. Since approval by OSHA wasn't a requirement for new construction or repair, only by the Fire Marshall or Arson, the rubble had already been cleared away. Only a gaping hole remained between the charred remains of the flanking homes. "Thanks to a faulty gas line, when the homeowner turned on her dryer, the explosion literally blew the roof off the back end of the house. By the time we arrived, the two surrounding structures were already fully consumed and the fire was spreading."

She consulted the incident report. "The homeowner didn't survive, is that correct?"

He shook his head. "She died during transport by the EMS team."

She hesitated, dreading the next question. The sounds from the construction crews restoring order filled the heavy silence that hung between her and Ben. "Would you show me which residence FF2 Fitzpatrick and FF1 Mitchell entered?"

Ben didn't speak, but turned and headed up the road. Four homes down he stopped. At the top of a long, sloped drive, stood the skeletal remains of a two-story home.

"According to the incident report, three of the residents were still inside the house." She pulled in a deep breath and forced herself to continue despite the heavy weight filling her heart at the thought of two small children and their mother trapped inside the burning house. "Do you know how that was possible when the entire neighborhood would've heard, and probably even felt, the explosion?"

"Drew could give you the specifics since he interviewed the mother," he said. "Apparently she slept through it and didn't wake up until she heard her kids screaming. She was trapped at one end of the second floor and her kids were down the hall in their bedrooms."

"What did you do once you became aware of the situation?"

He pulled his hands from his jacket and folded his arms across his chest. "I gave the order for the search and rescue, and sent in Fitz and Mitchell."

"Do you always apply the two-in/two-out rule during search-and-rescue operations?" A lame question, especially for a seasoned firefighter like Ben. Still, she had to ask, even if doing so made her feel like crap.

He shot a quick, impatient glance her way. "It is standard operating procedure."

She cleared her throat and studied her notes. "Fitzpatrick handed the little boy through the window to the team waiting, then Mitchell exited with the younger girl. Do you know why Mitchell would leave with the girl instead of remaining with Fitzpatrick?"

Ben raked his hand through his hair, then rubbed at the tension knotting the back of his neck. He knew the answer, but he hesitated, choosing his words carefully. Although Chance Mitchell lacked time on the job, he didn't fault the younger firefighter for his judgment; he'd followed protocol.

Although Fitz would occasionally act on instinct rather than procedure, he'd still been a good firefighter. Ben had been fully aware of those wild-card tendencies, but he also knew Fitz would give his own life before he'd leave another firefighter behind. The younger firefighters learned from the older ones. Until recently, Ben had never questioned the status quo, or believed it could end in disaster.

"Fitz was supposed to be behind Mitchell," he told

Jana. "But he went back for the mother instead. Flames had been spotted shooting from the roof of the structure, compromising scene safety. The horns were going off to signal immediate evacuation, so Mitchell *couldn't* go back for Fitz. We had to wait for RIT."

What Ben didn't tell Jana—or write in the reports—was that Mitchell had attempted to return for Fitz. In fact, it had taken Noah Harding and two members from another squad to keep Mitchell from running back into the house.

Just because Mitchell hadn't been allowed to help Fitz didn't mean he'd been derelict in his duties. Only the specially trained team could enter once the safety of the firefighters became an issue.

"Is there a reason RIT wasn't called in sooner?" she asked.

The officious tone of her voice bugged him. She was only doing her job, asking the hard questions, but that didn't quell the annoyance from seeping under his skin. "We had no knowledge that backdraft was about to happen," he explained. "As soon as I was notified Fitz hadn't come out, the team was summoned."

She held his gaze, her green eyes intent. "But the team never made it inside. Why?"

On a conscious level he understood her beleaguering him with questions was all part of the distasteful process. He knew she didn't enjoy forcing him to walk across emotional hot coals. It still didn't make it any easier.

"RIT started in," he said, his words sharp and

clipped. "They were called back because the structural integrity had been compromised."

She bent her head and scribbled something down. Reading upside down, he deciphered the notation 2x2 training. The words slammed into his guilt and pain, shoving them aside in favor of another round of impatience, all aimed at Jana and her determination to probe a gaping wound.

"Fitzpatrick saved the mother. Then the roof collapsed, trapping him inside," she said, stating the obvious. "The incident reports indicate that he radioed you that he was running out of air."

He braced his feet a slight distance apart and crossed his arms. "That's right."

The sharpness of his voice had her lowering her clipboard to look up at him and frown. "So he knew he only had so much air in his tank and he probably heard the horn blasts indicating immediate evacuation. But he still went back for the mother. Why?"

He let out a slow, ragged breath. "Fitz followed his instincts. That woman would've died, and he did what any one of us might have done. He made the save. Those kids have a mother today thanks to Fitz. That has to count for something."

Her frown deepened, and she shook her head. "No," she said emphatically. "It doesn't work that way."

The assignment of fault landed between them with a thud, only she hadn't placed it at his door. Fitz had screwed up by ignoring protocol, but he'd paid the price with his life, leaving behind a wife and two young sons to mourn the loss. Wasn't that payment enough without having his last act of duty and heroism labeled firefighter error?

"Don't be so quick to judge a situation you've never been in, Jana. Can you honestly tell me you might not have done the same thing in his situation?"

"No, I wouldn't have," she argued stubbornly. "True, I've never been faced with that kind of life-or-death choice. I'm not trying to downplay how difficult it would be to retreat from a burning building knowing there are people still inside, especially if you think there's the slimmest chance of saving them. But regulations are in place to prevent this kind of accident from occurring, and there's no denying Fitzpatrick ignored them. Yes, it cost him his life, but he selfishly risked the lives of everyone on the scene that day, too."

A thousand arguments sprang to mind, but Ben mentioned none. He couldn't after she'd stripped it all down to the basic, ugly truth. "I guess this means you'll be concluding the incident was a result of firefighter error."

She glanced over at what was left of the house, then back at him. "I have to, Ben." Her gaze filled with compassion. "Fitzpatrick disregarded his training. His impulsiveness risked lives. What if Mitchell had gone back inside that house? You would have buried two members of your squad instead of one. I'm very sorry for your loss, but you can't ignore the facts."

He wanted to hate her for voicing what he'd known all along, but he couldn't. Instead, he reminded himself that firefighter error in this instance wouldn't carry much weight with the squad. In their eyes, Fitz was a hero. Although Jana hadn't blamed him, that knowledge didn't end Ben's journey on the guilt-trip express. He'd been the one in charge that day. That's all that mattered in the end.

As he and Jana walked silently down the hill to their cars, morbid reflection took hold of him. This wasn't the first time he'd been affected by a ruling of firefighter error. The underlying cause of his mother's death had been determined as such. Unlike Fitz, the fault had not been assigned to Joanna Perry, but to the two firefighters sent in to save her once she'd become trapped inside a burning warehouse.

But he had no idea what had happened to one of the men who'd been sent in to retrieve his mom. Unfortunately, he couldn't say the same for the other. He and his brothers had been personally subjected to the fallout because their own father had been labeled a screwup of the worst kind.

SINCE RETURNING from the incident scene two days ago, Ben had remained true to his word and hadn't pressured Jana to get together once. If it hadn't been for the hungry look in his eyes when she'd arrived at the firehouse this morning, Jana might've wondered if he even wanted to see her again.

She didn't regret her decision that they keep their distance until she finished her job. Much. Although Ben had behaved like a perfect gentleman, she'd decided she'd rather face skydiving without a parachute before she'd ever admit she'd reached her limit. Thank heavens she would be wrapping up the investigation today.

Two and a half days of no sexy phone calls, no kissing and no orgasms had taken such a toll on her, she hovered dangerously close to the clinical definition of loony tunes.

She reexamined the rescue ropes Ben had laid out for her, then consulted the equipment checklist again. "This indicates a complete equipment inspection was performed over the weekend. Didn't anyone notice these ropes have flaws in the fiber? They should have been pulled and used as utility rope."

"A minor oversight," he said. "I'll have it corrected immediately."

She wasn't fooled by his bland expression, or by the threat of impatience in his voice he hadn't been able to mask today. She did experience a tiny twinge of guilt for not letting him know right away that this would be her last day at the firehouse, but misery loved a crowd and the party in her panties had been mighty dull.

She scanned her notes again. "There's a minor backup in the drain where the blood-borne pathogens are cleaned. It's not to the point where it's a health hazard, but it should be brought up to code fairly soon."

"Anything else?"

She glanced up at him and smiled when he frowned. "A couple of the men have stickers on their helmets. They are flammable and could cause a problem. It's not a violation, but it can affect the integrity of the helmet."

She set the clipboard on the worktable, then slowly peeled off her black-and-white checked blazer. The blue of his eyes darkened considerably as she intentionally thrust her breasts forward. Heat flared in his eyes, warming her from the inside out as he swept his gaze down the length of her.

She reached up to unfasten the top two buttons of her blouse. "Noah Harding's helmet has been slightly modified."

He shoved his hand roughly through his hair.

"Just make sure he corrects it immediately so it's OSHA compliant."

He merely nodded, making her wonder if she'd chased his vocal chords into hibernation with her quasi-striptease. Snatching her clipboard from the table, she scanned her checklist. "I need you to run a test on the thermal-imaging camera for me."

He spun around and crossed the quiet bay to the gleaming red fire truck parked inside. She struggled to maintain slow, even breaths instead of gasping for air like a fish. The cords and muscle of his forearms rippled when he pulled the TIC from the storage unit, magnifying exactly what she'd been missing the last couple of days—the feel of those strong arms holding her.

"Is this the same model Mitchell and Fitzpatrick had with them when they entered the premises?" she asked once she brought *her* vocal chords out of hibernation.

He flipped a switch on the side of the camera and it instantly whirred to life. "No. This is the latest model."

The price of moving in next to him was a quick succession of rapid heartbeats. Breathing in his rich, masculine scent nearly had her sighing with pleasure.

She caught herself before she made a fool of herself and revealed just how much abstinence was costing her—by the second. "Have you seen Drew today?" she asked abruptly.

He frowned. "What do you want with Drew?"

"I had a couple of questions about one of the witness statements he took at the scene," she explained. "Nothing major."

That deep frown of his eased somewhat. "He's taking a couple of extra days off to study for the Fire Detective's exam this weekend."

The news surprised her almost as much as the note of pride in his voice. She couldn't imagine Ben as anything other than a firefighter. The man was dedication to the badge personified. For that reason alone, she would've thought he'd have a strong opinion about his brother leaving the arson squad and defecting to the other side to join the police force formally.

She leaned closer to confirm the last inspection date on the heat sensor. Good grief, he smelled incredible. "All that's left is a quickie test," she said, "and we're done here."

A half smile tipped up one corner of his lips. "Sure all you want is a...quickie?"

The sexy innuendo taunted her thinly stretched limits, but she wasn't about to object now that the only thing standing between her and a night of hot, intense pleasure with Ben was an equipment test. "Ben." She wanted her tone to be warning, but it ended up breathless and needy. "Can we just do it now, please."

His smile shifted to an all-out wicked grin. Too late, she realized the double meaning behind her poorly—or maybe appropriately—chosen words. Her blood heated, especially when she caught sight of the desire in his eyes. The man was impossible to resist.

"The camera," she amended. "Can we test the camera, please?"

He made a minor adjustment then held the TIC so she could adequately assess the viewing screen once he pointed the lens at the door of the engine. She kept her attention on the small screen until the thermal image of his hand appeared in the viewer. With the tip of his middle finger, he wrote something on the door of the engine—I want you!

The words faded as the heat he'd transmitted cooled, but the images of erotic possibilities remained permanently etched in her mind. "How did you do that?" How did he make her so hot with only three thoroughly intoxicating words?

His smile was slow, lazy and filled with the promise of sin. "Body heat."

The low husky rumble of his voice had warmth pooling instantly in her belly, sinking lower and lower until an insistent, throbbing ache made her squirm. He put the camera away, then leaned against the side of the engine as if he hadn't just sent her body into sensory overload. Again.

The sexy cant of his mouth combined with the pure interest in his eyes snipped the final thread on her self-discipline. "Tonight?"

His eyebrows winged upward. "Are you sure?"

She nodded, encouraged by the hope in his voice. "My work here is almost done. I won't be back tomorrow."

"My place," he said, pushing off the engine. "Six-thirty. Sharp." He told her the address.

She wouldn't dream of arguing with him. "I'll bring dinner."

"And dessert?"

She gave him a long hard stare, then slowly smiled. "You're lookin' at it, babe."

11

BEN JUMPED DOWN from the engine, his attention already on the scene, assessing the situation. The front end of a silver, older-model sedan was crushed against a utility pole. Downed power lines, whether from the impact of the car or the horrendous thunderstorm, sparked and danced over the wet pavement. The extreme danger prevented the squad from freeing the unconscious woman trapped inside the vehicle.

He issued instructions, ordering the men to stand by until the safety officer declared the scene secure. Cale and Brady, the first to arrive, waited impatiently in the pouring rain for word they could approach the driver to determine the extent of her injuries above and beyond the obvious head trauma.

In Ben's experience, the first rain of the season ranked as one of the worst for creating traffic collisions. Highways and streets slick from summer oil residue and careless or impatient drivers ignoring road conditions made for a dangerous, and often deadly, combination. With the series of storms predicted to hit the California coastline only beginning, they were in for a long few days.

"What the hell is she doing here?" Noah Harding shouted above the din.

Ben followed Noah's line of vision and saw Jana crossing the street. His heart stopped, then resumed beating a rapid cadence in his chest. They had more than enough to deal with at the moment. Dammit, he couldn't afford Jana as a distraction.

"Being a pain in the ass," Chance Mitchell answered, shaking his head.

Ben silently agreed with him, but he wouldn't undermine Jana's authority by saying so. "She's doing her job," he told the two younger firefighters. "And I expect you to do yours and not worry about OSHA observing. Got it?"

Having an OSHA rep on scene to observe wasn't unusual when a department was under investigation. But seeing Jana unnerved him.

She'd nearly made it across the busy roadway before one of the cops directing traffic away from the area attempted to stop her. She said something Ben couldn't make out, flashed her credentials, then dismissed the cop and headed straight for him.

"See what's taking the power company so long." He issued the order to Noah, then took off before Jana closed in on him and his men.

Not thirty minutes ago he'd been swept up by a rampant case of lust. He hadn't been certain he'd even survive the next three hours before he'd have her in his arms—and in his bed—again. Right this second, though, he wanted nothing more than to ream her a new one for her total disregard for her own safety by approaching a dangerous situation.

Counting to ten before he caught up with her did

zilch to calm him. "What the hell do you think you're doing?" he snapped.

She blinked her wet spiky lashes several times, obviously surprised by his surly attitude after their exchange back at the firehouse. He didn't want her injured at the scene, so he figured he was entitled.

"I have every right to be here." She held the front of her trench coat together by wrapping her arms around her waist.

"Dammit, Jana, you could get hurt."

Or worse. The thought filled him with a different kind of dread he'd never experienced until now. Until her. He'd been taking care of people for as long as he could remember. His brothers and Tilly had done their share of rattling his cage with their juvenile antics, but that was next to nothing compared to the way his heart had stopped beating when he thought about what could happen if those live wires got out of control.

"Don't waste time by yelling at me, Ben. Just apprise me of the situation."

He let out a rough sigh. She had a point. "Vehicle versus utility pole," he said. "The driver appears injured and unconscious."

Loud snaps of high-voltage electricity rent the air with a distinct acrid scent. Shouts from the emergency personnel on the scene had him not waiting around for more of her questions, but rushing back to the action circle.

The power lines danced around the vehicle, jerking over the ground, setting off showers of sparks. The driver remained unconscious, oblivious of the extreme

danger surrounding her. Ben reminded his men to stay
clear, knowing firsthand how helpless and frustrated
they were feeling, forced to wait to do what they'd been
trained for—saving lives.

"Oh, my God," Jana gasped from beside him. "She's
pregnant."

He hadn't even heard her approach, and he certainly
hadn't heard her correctly. At least he hoped not.
"What did you just say?"

"She's pregnant," she repeated, pointing toward
what was left of the silver sedan.

He hadn't even realized, but with a better look, he
confirmed Jana's observation. The driver's large,
rounded belly was wedged against the bent steering
wheel. No air bag had deployed, likely due to the age of
the car.

Noah approached and ignored Jana. "The power
company's ETA is at least ten minutes," he told Ben.

That was not good news. "What's the holdup? Did
you remind them this is a priority-one situation?"

Noah nodded. "Traffic. Rain. Power outage on the
other end of town," he said. "Take your pick."

"Stay here," he ordered Jana. "Better yet, move
back."

He didn't wait to see if she obeyed, but went to speak
to Cale and Brady. "Did you notice the driver's pregnant?"

Brady was visibly pale. "Yeah, we noticed."

"I could try to get to her from the other side," Cale
told Ben. "Maybe break through the sunroof."

Ben gave his brother a harsh look. "With live wires

down? Think again. We wait for the power company. Understood?"

Cale's expression remained grim, but he didn't argue.

Jana rushed toward them. "You have to do something." A slice of panic filled her voice. One look at her told him she was teetering on the verge of hysteria. "Why aren't you doing something?"

He needed her out of the way and to calm down before she did something stupid and dangerous. "I thought I told you to get back." he reminded her, keeping his tone as gentle as possible.

"You have to get that woman out of there." Her wide eyes were banked with fear. "What if there's a leak in the gas line?"

The sparks could set off an explosion, and they all knew it, but their hands were tied. The power lines snapped and popped again, shooting a fresh shower of sparks over the top of the vehicle.

Jana flinched, and he knew he'd better put as much distance between her and the scene as possible, fast. If the situation worsened, he didn't want to think about how it might affect her. The squad had the benefit of the critical-incident stress-debriefing team, a luxury Jana wouldn't have at her disposal.

Settling his hands on her shoulders, he steered her away from the action and led her to the side of Cale and Brady's rig, opened the passenger door and helped her inside. For once, she didn't argue with him.

"You have to help that woman," she said again. "You have to save her and her baby."

He reached around her, pulled a blanket from the bin behind the seat and tucked it around her legs. "We will. I promise."

Her cold fingers slid over his cheeks and she forced him to look at her. "Do something, Ben. Do it now."

"We have to wait for the utility company first." He used the same quiet tone he reserved for panicked victims as he reached up to pull her hands away and settle them on her lap. "It's not safe for us to work until they kill those power lines."

Did she realize the irony of the situation? he wondered. Emergencies took on a whole new perspective when actual humans were involved. Something no textbook had prepared her to handle on such a personal level.

The warmth of the ambulance must've penetrated her skin because she shivered.

"As soon as the scene is safe, Cale and Brady will be able to go in and assess her injuries. It won't be much longer." He hoped.

Her bottom lip quivered and she trembled again. There were more shouts, but he forced himself to ignore them for the next few seconds while he helped Jana relax.

He slipped a damp lock of hair behind her ear. "I need you to stay here," he told her. "No matter what happens, okay?"

Her green eyes filled with moisture, and she nodded. His chest squeezed so tight, drawing his next breath took enormous concentration. Somehow he'd landed neck-deep in big trouble. As much as he would've liked to deny the truth, he couldn't ignore the realization that Jana was becoming important to him.

He'd enjoyed her body and had taken pleasure in the intimacy of her passionate response as a lover. Her teasing and flirting never failed to make him want her more. He'd even argued with her and felt the sting of frustration with her stubbornness. Her smiles always kicked his pulse up a few notches. A sultry glance or a gentle touch from her effortlessly set him on fire. All understandable and acceptable responses. Yet none of the facets of her personality he'd witnessed thus far had prepared him for his reaction to the stark vulnerability in her gaze.

He couldn't do this now. There was work to be done, but heaven help him, all he wanted was to hold her close and keep her safe.

For as long as she'd have him? Or a whole lot longer?

The arrival of the utility company's emergency crew offered him a temporary reprieve from further exploration of the emotions crowding him. At least for the moment. Later, he wouldn't be as fortunate.

JANA PLUCKED Ben's shirt from the floor and adjusted it around her shoulders to ward off the slight chill in the room. She'd all but torn it off his incredible body when she got to his place and was surprised now to see the buttons still intact.

She'd been thirty minutes late because she'd had difficulty reading the directions he'd given her; they'd been soaked from being in her coat pocket. By the time she'd finally arrived, she'd been starved—for him.

She'd hardly made it through the wide arched doorway before she'd wrapped herself around him and held on tight. The afternoon had been highly emotional, and she still had trouble pinpointing what she was feeling right now, a suitable excuse for her practically attacking the poor guy the second she walked in the door.

Not that he'd complained, she thought, hiding a smile as she rolled back the sleeves of his shirt. He'd let her set the pace, almost as if he'd known she needed to be the one in absolute control. She'd been frantic to have him inside her. They'd never made it to his bedroom, but had made love in the middle of his livingroom floor. Afterward, he'd taken her to his bed where he'd been gentle and so caring, her heart still ached just thinking about the tender way he'd loved her.

She looked up as he returned with a bed tray loaded with cartons of Chinese takeout. After settling the tray in the middle of the bed, he joined her and opened the boxes to let the steam escape.

She crossed her legs and tore off the wrapper on a pair of chopsticks. "I have a whole new respect for you," she said.

He held up the takeout carton filled with steaming lo mien for her. "I was that good, huh?"

She laughed as she plucked a piece of chicken from the container, then leaned over and planted a quick kiss on his lips. "Your skills in that department are exemplary," she said. "What I meant was that in an official capacity, it's real easy for me to say the rules must be followed no matter what. I've been taught that if the scene isn't safe, you can't help someone because the danger would place more lives at risk. But reality is way different, and I lost it out there. I wasn't prepared for that kind of emotional intensity. How do you do it day after day?"

He settled his hand over her knee. "It's not easy, but that's where experience makes a difference." Using a fork rather than chopsticks, he dug into the carton for lo-mien noodles. "It's not exactly something you learn from a book, is it?"

She praised the invention of the microwave oven as she bit into the warm, moist chicken—they'd had to re-heat it since they'd started with dessert. Twice.

"No," she admitted. With monumental effort, she had kept her word that afternoon and had remained in the ambulance as she'd promised Ben. Although, she *had* climbed over to the driver's seat for a better view. "It isn't."

Once the power company personnel had finally ar-rived to handle the power lines and declared the scene safe, the men under Ben's command had worked swiftly and efficiently as a team. They'd freed the driver so Cale and his partner could assess her injuries, then stabilize and transport the woman to the emergency room. The baby had seemed fine, but Cale had told Jana before they'd left the scene that, in addition to the head injury, the driver had suffered a broken ankle and wrist. Ben had spoken to Cale later before leaving the firehouse, and had learned there weren't any other complications.

"I watched you with the men," she said. "You really do look out for their safety while they do their jobs."

She couldn't help but admire him. He guided his men based on instinct, not impulse, which added to the deep respect he already held in her eyes, not only as a fire-fighter, but as a man. He was kind, compassionate and when she'd been busy this past week conducting inter-views, inspecting ropes and drainage systems, and gen-erally giving him a hard time, he'd sneaked right into her heart. "Do you realize you're a natural?" she asked him.

A natural heartbreaker? she wondered. She hoped not, but she knew that once their fling ran its course, someone would end up with a broken heart. And it probably wouldn't be him.

His lips quirked slightly. "Runs in the family, I guess. My folks were with the department."

She snagged the carton of fried rice from the metal tray resting near her hip. "They must be really proud of you and your brothers."

"I'd like to think they would've been," he said ab-sently, concentrating on the carton of lo mien.

He lay down casually on his side, propping himself up with his elbow, the dark blue sheet draped over him to his waist. Despite his laid-back appearance, she sensed a forced note of dispassion in his voice.

Her curiosity got the better of her. "Would've been?" she prompted.

"My mom died when I was ten." His shoulders visi-bly tensed. "My old man went about two years later."

"I'm sorry," she said quietly. Her parents drove her nuts, but they were around. Sort of.

"It was a long time ago," he said, still not looking at her.

Chopsticks and rice were a messy combination, especially in bed, so she exchanged fried rice for shrimp and snow peas. "It had to be hard on you." She kept her tone casual while rooting through the snow peas for shrimp. "On all of you," she added and stole a peek at him.

"Subtlety is not one of your stronger points, babe." The hint of a smirk tilted his lips. "If you want to know what happened, just ask me."

Bingo! Shrimp at last. "Tell me about your parents," she said, then popped a fat piece of seafood into her mouth.

He leaned over and poked his fork inside the container in her hands. "I'll show you mine if you show me yours."

She giggled and rolled her eyes. "Oh, yeah, and you're such a master of subtlety."

"For that, you have to go first."

"Ha! I asked first."

"So," he said, then took a bite of the food he'd piled onto his fork.

At the rate he was stalling, she'd end up missing her flight in the morning before she learned anything about his past. She was booked on the 5:00 a.m. commuter flight to San Jose where she'd pick up a rental car and drive to Carmel for the training session Gwen had asked her to attend. Originally, Jana had planned to return to L.A. immediately, but after the tension of this afternoon, she'd changed her mind and decided to take advantage of the peace and tranquility of the white-sand beaches of Carmel.

"My parents divorced when I was in high school," she told him. "My dad's work takes him out of town for long periods of time and he was never around much, so it's not as if it was some huge, traumatic event in my life. Actually, it was more of a relief when they finally did divorce."

Curiosity filled his gaze. "Why a relief?"

"They fought constantly."

"Because of his job?"

Jana plucked more shrimp from the carton and considered her answer. "Not exactly," she said, then let out a long, slow breath. "Usually they fought because my mom heard about one of his affairs. The concept of discretion is lost on my father. Okay. Your turn."

"Uh-uh." He reached over and snatched the container from her hand. "And no more shrimp until you tell me more."

She shoved the sleeves of the shirt up her arms, and gave him a glare filled with mock indignation. "Now you have definitely gone too far. Didn't anyone ever tell you never to separate a woman from her shrimp?"

He passed the carton in front of her nose. "Hmm, smells good, does it?"

The sleeves snaked back down her arms and she blew out a stream of breath. "My dad's a film director, documentaries, mostly. His work meant more to him than his family and it caused problems."

One of his eyebrows winged up at the bitterness in her voice. She couldn't help it—she had baggage. And she'd not only dragged it out for his inspection, she'd even managed to trip over it and land flat on her face. "Now can I have my shrimp, please?"

He smiled. "One more question."

She shook her head and held out her hand. "It's your turn. Shrimp please."

Ben reluctantly handed Jana the carton of food. He didn't exactly dread the questions he knew were coming, but he very rarely discussed childhood. He hardly ever spoke of the past with his own brothers, and never once had he shared the ugliness of it all with a woman. His aunt had paid for the best child psychologists money could buy for him and his brothers after their dad had passed away. As far as he was concerned, he'd dealt with it once. There was no worthwhile reason he could see in rehashing the past.

"My mom was a firefighter," he said, as if they were discussing nothing more dramatic than the change in the weather. "She lost her life on the job. My dad couldn't take it, fell apart and died a couple of years later from a massive coronary."

Jana tilted her head and regarded him quizzically. "That was a very cool response for someone who lost his parents at such a young age."

He set his fork on the tray and shrugged. "Bad things happen to good people, Jana. When they do, you have two choices. Deal with it and move on, or let it eat at you like my dad did until there's nothing left. I'm not my dad."

A frown creased her forehead as she started clearing

away the cartons. "You've moved on?" she questioned. "Or just avoided the subject by ignoring it?"

He took the tray from her and set it on the floor. "Moved on," he stated firmly. His brothers had needed him to be strong so he hadn't been able to lose it.

He settled back on the bed beside her and pulled her close. Because he needed the comfort of her touch? "I'm not saying it was a picnic," he admitted. "There was a lot going on between my folks before my mom died that Cale and Drew never knew about. My dad could be a real bastard, and he resented my mom because she'd joined the department. The county had tried to make her work EMS, but she'd trained to become a firefighter. She fought them and won, but it made things at home worse."

Jana snuggled against him, her head resting against his shoulder. God, he really could get used to this, he thought. Too bad it'd never last. Once she caught on that he could be as much of a bastard as his old man, all that would be left would be a vapor trail as she raced for the door.

"After she died, the guilt ate at him. He tried to avoid it by diving into a bottle of gin, but it didn't help. He'd rant and rave, or mumble to himself in a stupor. Once he told me that God took her because she chose her career over her children."

"Oh, Ben," she gasped. Her arm tightened around his waist. "That's an awful thing to say to a child. My parents argued, but they never brought us into their disagreements. I just can't imagine—"

"What it'd be like?" When she nodded, he said, "It

was rough on all of us, I won't deny that. I tried to keep the worst of it away from my brothers, especially when the old man would start drinking around the clock."

She tipped her head back to look at him. "You were only ten years old." Compassion filled her eyes. "How much did you really think you were capable of at that age?"

More than she'd ever know. He'd done things he wasn't particularly proud of to protect Cale and Drew. He hadn't practiced in a very long while, but he'd be willing to bet he could still flawlessly forge the old man's signature. He'd written checks and signed his father's name to keep the utility companies from disconnecting services and to deposit the payments from his mom's life insurance. He'd signed report cards and field-trip permission slips for himself and his brothers. The birth of automated tellers made it even easier for him to get cash so he wouldn't run the risk of getting busted. Those days hardly qualified as his best moments, but he'd done whatever was necessary to make sure they'd survived.

"I kept my brothers safe," he told her, suddenly way too anxious to change the subject for someone claiming he'd moved on and didn't dwell on the past. "Why are we discussing ancient history when there are so many more interesting things we could be doing?"

Memory lane held too many potholes. One wrong turn and the results could be as jarring as the realization that he'd willingly taken Jana down a path no other woman had ever traveled with him.

She looked at him, a seductive smile slowly curving her lips. "What'd you have in mind?"

He welcomed the diversion by urging her onto his lap. Without an ounce of hesitation, she straddled his hips. His body instantly responded. "Didn't you say something about dessert?"

The sound of her laughter did wonders in keeping the demons locked inside the closet where they belonged. No, he amended. There weren't any demons. He'd slain those dragons years ago. Hadn't he?

"Excuse me," she said, "but I seem to recall we've already had *that* dessert. A couple of servings, too."

He reached behind her, wrapped his hands in the silky strands of her hair, then gently tipped her head backward to expose her throat. "Appetizers," he said, then lowered his head to taste her satiny skin. Her breathy sigh heated his blood. Would he ever get enough of this woman? He was beginning to think not in a hundred years.

Her sultry moan coalesced with the sound of the tones from his beeper sounding off. He lifted his head and picked up his pager to read the lighted message. Multiple MVA with rollover and fire.

He had Jana off his lap before checking the location. "I've got to go," he said, turning on the bedside lamp to search for his briefs.

"Now?"

He scooped up his briefs, ignoring the disappointment in Jana's voice. He snagged his jeans, yanked them on and headed to the closet for a shirt.

The sheets rustled and the springs squeaked as she slipped from the bed. "Aren't you off duty?"

He grabbed the first shirt his fingers touched and tugged it over his head. "They're going to need me out there. I have to go." He fastened up his jeans and yanked open the drawer holding his socks. "Stay here and catch some sleep."

She picked up his boots and handed them to him. "I won't be here when you get back."

He glanced up, expecting to see displeasure in her eyes although he hadn't caught so much as a hint of censure in her voice. "I'll be back as soon as I can," he said impatiently, unwilling to buy into whatever guilt trip she planned to lay on him just because he was leaving her to do his job.

"It's already past midnight and I have a flight to catch in a few hours. My bag is already in the car. I'll be home Sunday around noon."

He stood and walked to the nightstand for his pager. "Where are you going?" he asked, more out of courtesy than any deep, burning desire to know her whereabouts. His mind was already on the possible complications he'd be facing once he reached the scene.

"Carmel for a weekend seminar."

He nodded absently and shrugged into his jacket. The words *weekend* and *seminar* penetrated as he started for the door.

"Aren't you forgetting something?"

Impatience nipped at him as he turned to face her. Didn't she realize he needed to hurry?

She held his keys in the palm of her hand, a gentle

smile on her face as she walked toward him. "You might need these."

He let out a breath of impatience. "Thanks. I'll call you later."

Without waiting for a reply, he was out the door, adrenaline pumping through his veins.

12

THE EARLY STORMS hammering the California coastline hadn't eased in two days, keeping all but the most diehard tourists at bay. The quaint seaside shopping village had been reduced to a virtual ghost town. Since spending time on the white-sand beaches was now out of the question due to the inclement weather, Jana spent the afternoon wandering from shop to shop in Carmel's quiet downtown district.

The occupational safety seminar had actually been quite informative. How could a weekend possibly be a total loss when she'd not only expanded her knowledge, but even lucked out by managing some early Christmas shopping? Unearthing an artist's print Chloe had mentioned she'd wanted for her office, and a beautiful set of antique crystal candleholders for Lauren almost made Jana's decision to remain for the weekend worthwhile.

She paid the clerk for the cappuccino and biscotti she'd ordered and carried them to the small table near the window to watch the rain. Awnings and overhangs from the buildings would've kept her relatively dry on the walk back to the hotel, but the wind had picked up again so she'd darted into the coffeehouse to wait out the sudden cloudburst.

She set her packages on one of the spare chairs, shrugged out of her coat and pulled her cell phone out of her purse to check her voice mail. Two messages waiting. She smiled at the excitement in Lauren's voice as her friend bubbled with the news that she'd been offered the female voice lead in the animated feature.

The other message was from her father, calling to confirm her attendance at the private screening of his newest documentary. Actually, it was her father's assistant who'd called, but to Jana, they were one and the same. She knew she needed to RSVP, but she hadn't made a decision about attending what would be the standard, over-the-top affair. An intimate gathering of family and friends, the formal invitation had stated. Her father's concept of *intimate* was anything less than forty industry professionals. Family was a definite afterthought.

The invitation had also stated she could bring a guest. Would Ben be interested in going with her? Without his pager?

She checked for text messages, but there were none. The sting of disappointment pierced her. Ben hadn't called as promised. After slipping her cell phone back into her bag, she took a tentative sip of cappuccino. She'd left her cell-phone number and the number of the hotel taped to his pillow before heading out for the airport before dawn Friday morning, but she hadn't heard a word from him. With the bad weather and probably dozens of traffic accidents and other emergencies, she assumed he'd be incredibly busy, and no doubt exhausted until the storms ended.

Logically, she understood. Emotionally, she worried. Not just about him and the dangers he could be facing, but also about their relationship. How on earth had she fallen so completely in love with him in so short a time?

A lot of reasons, she thought, and not all of them involved the bedroom. From her initial interviews with the men on his team, she'd been left with the impression Ben could be rather cold and detached at times. Efficient and in control, yes, she'd found, but never cold or detached. At least he hadn't been with her. When he wasn't behaving like a bullheaded moron insistent on getting his way, warm, kind and incredibly passionate were more apt descriptions she'd apply to his personality. He had an adorable sense of humor and made her laugh—often. There was a gentleness about him that drew her to him, as well. Combine all those traits with his deep respect for others around him, and all in all, there wasn't much about Ben not to love.

Still, she harbored reservations. One in particular.

On two separate occasions, he'd run out on her because his beeper had gone off. If he'd been on call, she might not be concerned, but he'd been off duty both times. Was she being selfish, or did she have cause for alarm?

Ben's job was important, that she couldn't deny. He saved lives. The men he worked with, the victims he helped save, depended on him. Unlike her workaholic father, Ben wasn't halfway around the world on location for months at a time, never giving his family a second thought. What Ben did mattered. Or could he be even more obsessed with his work than her father was, just in a different way?

Unsure of the answer, she dipped the edge of biscotti in her cappuccino to soften it. The one constant in her life had always been her mother. She hadn't exactly been a PTA, cookie-baking type of mom, but no event in the lives of her four daughters had ever been insignificant to her. All Jana had ever gotten out of her father by way of attention had been a string of gifts she suspected were actually from her mother to make up for his disinterest. The way Ben had taken care of his brothers told Jana family meant a great deal to him.

If she'd learned anything from her childhood, it was what she didn't want, and that was to be a single parent in a two-parent household. As a kid, she'd mistakenly assumed unwarranted blame for her dad's long absences and indifference. Her moment of profound realization had come in high school when she and Lauren had met Chloe Montgomery.

Chloe had transferred to Beverly Hills High School from Atlanta, Georgia, when her family had relocated to California because her dad had been hired by a high-powered law firm to head up its entertainment-law division. Chloe's childhood was logistically similar to Jana's and Lauren's, except their new friend had developed a more pragmatic approach toward her absent father than either Jana or Lauren had. In Chloe's opinion, constantly being disappointed because the person you kept trying to set on a pedestal always fell was a waste of energy. Accepting the reality that people in general were severely flawed was a much healthier response. Life was not a thirty-minute sitcom, she'd say.

Jana hadn't completely bought into the "severely flawed" aspect of Chloe's philosophy, but she'd definitely decided to stop wasting energy on a lost cause. The only way she'd put an end to the cycle would be if she stopped wanting her father to be something he simply wasn't capable of being. Either she could accept that truth or be miserable most of the time. She'd opted for acceptance.

By the time Jana finished off the last of her cappuccino, the downpour had diminished to a steady sprinkle. Deciding she'd make it back to the hotel without drowning, she gathered her packages and left the coffeehouse.

Ten minutes later, and only half-drowned, she slipped the electronic key into the slot and let herself into her room. She carefully set the packages on the floor of the compact closet, hung her wet coat in the bathroom to dry and considered her options for the remainder of the weekend. Leaving a day early certainly appealed to her, but only because she missed Ben. Although, she reminded herself as she slipped off her loafers, he hadn't even bothered to call. Still, so much as a hint from him that he missed her and she'd be on the next flight to L.A., no questions asked.

She towel-dried her hair and ran a comb through it, deciding room service and an in-room movie would have to suffice. "What a pitiful substitute for a night of hot and steamy sex with one buff firefighter," she said to her reflection.

She left the combination entry/closet/bathroom area and walked into the room—and screeched in fright.

There was a naked man in her bed. At least she was pretty sure he was naked since the sheets covered the essentials.

"What are you doing here, Ben?" she demanded once her heart slid from her throat back to her chest. Not exactly the welcome he'd probably hoped for, but he'd scared the life out of her.

"Buff, huh?"

She was thinking slimier than llama spit applied because he'd nearly given her a coronary. Although, he did look mighty scrumptious resting against the headboard, naked and ready.

She folded her arms and glared at him, determined not to be swayed by the tempting tilt of his mouth until he answered her question. "Better yet, how many laws did you break to get inside my room?"

"At least two or three," he said without an ounce of shame.

"I could have you arrested."

The scoundrel's grin deepened. "You won't."

She narrowed her eyes. "Don't be so sure of yourself."

"Then you'd have to settle for a pitiful substitute." The gentle, teasing light in his eyes weakened her knees. "I would think you'd prefer a night of hot and steamy sex."

Llama spit, she decided, had been a compliment. "Watching you being dragged from my room by a pair of burly cops has a certain appeal."

He chuckled. "Naaah."

All that overblown arrogance of his *almost* made her smile.

She made a sound of bogus disgust, crossed the room to the tapestry wing chair in the corner and sat. On the round rosewood table she noticed a vase filled with a dozen blush-colored roses that hadn't been there when she'd left her room earlier to go shopping.

"Don't think for a minute flowers are going to get you off the hook for scaring me half to death." She plucked one from the vase and inhaled the sweet scent. "So how *did* you get inside my room?" she asked, more out of curiosity than to follow through on an empty threat to have him arrested for breaking and entering.

"You weren't in, so I ordered roses, hoping they'd be delivered to your room right away. They were, and I just followed the bellman, waited until he was coming out and I walked in as if I belonged here." He frowned slightly. "The guy even wormed a tip out of me."

Naked, resourceful and arrogant. A definitely lethal combination for a woman falling head over heels in love. "I thought there were laws about this kind of thing," she said, not yet willing to feed his mammoth ego by letting on how thrilled she really was to see him.

A frown touched his brow. "If not, there should be," he said seriously. "You wouldn't believe how easy it was."

She twirled the rose between her fingers. "I suppose I could let you stay. After all, you don't appear to have any clothes and it is raining."

"I'd probably catch a cold."

"Or worse," she said as she stood and slowly walked toward him. "Pneumonia."

His smile returned. "Think of the guilt."

"So what do you suggest I do with you now that you're here?" She carefully peeled back the bedclothes. The air rushed out of her lungs at the sight of all that glorious bare skin at her disposal.

He snagged her hand and tugged her down beside him. Before she could catch her breath, he shifted his weight and had her beneath him. "I'm sure if you try real hard," he whispered, his breath hot against her ear, "you'll think of something."

She slipped her arms around him and held him close. "Thinking," she said, "isn't quite what I have in mind."

NIGHT HAD FALLEN by the time they'd finally surfaced for air four hours later. Since there'd finally been a break in the storm, they'd ventured from the room for a late supper. The Italian restaurant was a total cliché and utterly charming, complete with drippy candles, red-and-white checkerboard tablecloths and a Frank Sinatra CD playing softly in the background.

Over a dinner of shrimp scampi and angel hair pasta, she'd discovered Ben was conservative with borderline liberal tendencies, something she decided her bleeding-heart views could tolerate. He'd also confirmed there weren't any junior studs running around wanting to be just like their daddy, either, although she'd figured that one out on her own after having been to his place. What did surprise her, though, was that he'd never been close to marriage, which made her wonder about his ability to commit to a long-term relationship.

"Not once?" she asked him, certain his single status hadn't stemmed from lack of female companionship. "Not even close?"

He shook his head and took a deep drink of the dark red wine they'd ordered with dinner. "Not even close," he said.

"I was. Not engaged, but almost," she admitted. "We were in college and when he transferred to Florida State, I learned that everything they say about the survival rate of long-distance relationships is true."

A wicked smile suddenly tugged his lips. "Tell me your fantasy," he whispered, leaning close.

She probably should consider his abrupt change in subject as a warning signal of some kind, but the intensity of his eyes as he waited for an answer ceased all rational thought. "Unexplored terrain," she answered sheepishly. She offered him a helpless shrug. "Sorry."

If she'd surprised him, he hid it well. "Everyone has fantasies," he said, a coaxing tone to his voice. His hand settled just above her knee, beneath the hem of her short red skirt.

Her skin heated. "Not everyone." She had memories, not fantasies. Delicious, sexy memories of their lovemaking.

"I fantasize about you." His hand crept under the hem of her skirt, far enough that his fingers teased her exposed skin above the lacy tops of her stockings. "A lot."

She dragged much-needed oxygen into her lungs and

prayed the length of the tablecloth would prevent any-one from discovering them pushing the intimacy enve-lope.

"Really?" Not that she needed an explanation. Her memory was doing an excellent job all on its own.

He nodded and held her captive with his gaze. "Ear-lier," he said quietly. "In the shower."

She cleared her throat as the sensual flashbacks clam-ored for attention. "Uh, that wasn't exactly a fantasy," she whispered. More like one-hundred percent, authen-tic lovemaking. Her body tingled as she recalled how their bodies, slick from soap and steamy water, had come together in an explosion of need. Hot. Aban-doned. And wickedly yummy.

His hand moved over her skin to massage her inner thigh. "That was a fantasy," he said as he gently urged her legs apart. "One I've had about you for a while."

A groan bubbled up inside her when the tips of his fingers feathered intimately over her panties. She let out a slow hiss of breath, convinced fantasy paled in com-parison to her current reality.

He leaned closer, as if attempting to shield her from the view of the few patrons in the restaurant. Thank heavens he'd selected a booth in a dark corner. Inten-tionally? she wondered. Considering he'd already proven the extent of his resourcefulness, she wouldn't put it past him.

"Have you ever pleasured yourself, Jana?" he whis-pered in her ear.

Electrifying shocks skittered over her skin. "Until a

week ago, I'd never had an orgasm. What do you think?"

He pulled back to look at her. Desire, rather than disappointment, darkened his eyes. "What about that night on the phone?"

She shook her head. "Nope." But, oh, had she ever ached for him.

"Do you trust me?" he asked her after a moment.

Physically he'd never harm her, she knew that as much as she knew the sun would rise in the east and set in the west until the end of time. Did she trust him not to break her heart? Not within a centimeter of his life.

"Yes," she whispered. "I trust you."

"Close your eyes."

"In case you've forgotten, we are in a restaurant," she said, but did as he asked anyway. "A public restaurant."

"Tell me what you're wearing—beneath your clothes."

Location obviously meant little to a man intent on a path of seduction. "Panties and a bra."

"That's not very imaginative. What color are they?"

"Red. Like the color of ripe, juicy cherries," she elaborated for him. "Or a velvet box of Valentine candy." She opened one eye to look at him. "Or the color of my cheeks?"

His fingers stilled, and he chuckled. "Close your eyes."

She did and felt his fingers brush lightly over her panties again. Like a junkie needing a fix, she leaned into his touch as if it were a drug that would take her into the sexual fantasy he was creating for her.

"You're wearing lace."

His deep, husky voice intoxicated her. His caress excited her.

"Is it a thong?" he asked. "Is the thin scrap of material massaging you, lightly teasing you so you're becoming swollen? Wet? Waiting for my touch?"

In her mind, she envisioned the length of his fingers exploring her deeply. Hot, blazing desire rushed through her veins like water bursting through a dam. "Ben." The whisper of his name sounded more like a whimper of need.

"Tell me what kind of panties you're wearing, Jana. I'll know if you lie."

The pad of his thumb traced a slow and rhythmic pattern around her folds. In her fantasy, the moist heat of his mouth closed over her. "They're boy shorts."

"Hmm," he murmured. "They're damp. That makes me hot."

She bit her lip when her mind conjured the image of his teeth gently grazing her while his tongue lapped at her. The restaurant faded away and they were in a secluded cove. The only thing between their bodies and the white sands of the beach was a blanket. Waves crashed against the shore in the distance as the sun kissed their bodies, and he kissed her intimately.

The first knot of tension tightened in her belly. Then another and another.

They were hedonistic sea nymphs. Naked and

naughty, where nothing mattered except the pleasure of their bodies.

She was Botticelli's Venus. Newly born and free to explore the pleasures of her body without constraint.

She was about to have an orgasm right in the middle of a restaurant!

Her eyes flew open, and she grabbed his wrist to urge him away from her before the world exploded. "We have to leave," she told him, her voice tight with strain.

"Why?" he asked with feigned innocence. His gaze held hers as he pressed his hand against her with perfect tension-building precision. She squirmed beneath his touch. "You're just getting started."

Her fingers trembled as she reached for her forgotten glass of wine, draining the contents as if it were nothing more potent than tap water. "Ben," she said as another tremor threatened to rock her. "If you don't get me out of here now, I'm going to come right here."

13

"IF YOU DON'T KNOW your body intimately," Ben said, "then how do you expect to know what gives you pleasure?"

With her back against his chest, Ben held Jana's gaze as they stood facing the full-length mirror of the sliding closet door. Their images were bathed in soft light from the bedside lamp in the other room, reminding him of a shadowed sensual portrait.

A sultry smile lifted her mouth. "Oh, I know what pleases me."

He smoothed his hands down her arms. "Then tell me. What makes you fall apart?"

Apprehension filled her eyes. "Isn't it obvious? You know, when I...when you make me..." She shrugged. *"You know."*

A slight blush tinged her cheeks. He bit back a smile at her sudden bout of shyness. Less than half an hour ago in the restaurant, she hadn't shown him an ounce of timidity when she'd announced exactly how close she'd been to orgasm.

His ploy to distract her from the uncomfortable subject of past relationships rated as a success, even if the solution had left him close to the brink himself. A punishment he fully deserved, he supposed, but the situation had called for drastic measures. He just hadn't realized how much physical pain his act of desperation would cost him.

The red stretchy lace of her panties rode low across her hips and barely covered the delectable curve of her bottom. The swell of her breasts rose and fell above a matching lace bra that left very little to his overactive imagination. He had absolutely no objections.

He covered her dainty, delicate hands with his much larger ones, slowly gliding them over the swell of her hips. His fingertips traced her skin, soft, silky and warm to the touch. "I want you to feel what I do when I touch you." He dipped his head and nipped gently at her shoulder. "Know what makes your body respond. What brings you close to the edge and what it takes to send you flying over the side."

"Ben?" Apprehension laced her whispered voice.

He kissed the side of her neck. "Shhh," he murmured. "Just open your mind to the possibilities."

A night of sensual self-discovery required her absolute willingness to accompany him on the journey. Whether or not she realized it, she'd been gifting him with her trust from the moment they'd first met. Tonight, they'd test the limits. No reservations. No regrets. No holding back. Tonight, he wanted all of her.

Could he accept, without reservation or regret, the precious commodity he demanded from her? He hadn't lied when he'd told her he'd never been close to marriage. The mere thought of a lifetime commitment usually gave him hives. While he wasn't exactly ready to ask Jana to add Perry to her last name, he was highly suspicious of the stark loneliness that had hit him hard when he'd returned home to an empty house early this morning.

He'd gone on several runs after he'd left Jana on Thursday night, and had ended up bunking down at the firehouse to catch an hour or two of sleep before his regular shift on Friday. The squad had been ungodly busy with one call after another, and he'd put in another eighteen hours. When he'd started barking orders like an angry drill sergeant, the captain had had enough of him and threatened a week's suspension if he showed his face at the firehouse before Monday morning. Ben didn't believe Rick would actually suspend him, but when he started snapping at the squad from sheer exhaustion, he knew he'd better take a serious break before he completely alienated his men.

At first he'd convinced himself the only reason he'd decided to surprise Jana was to ensure he kept his distance from the firehouse for the next couple of days. This belief had been shattered by the sweet sound of her voice when she hadn't yet realized he'd gotten into her hotel room. He *had* longed to be with her, sure, but how easily he'd accepted that knowledge made him think he should start checking for big red bumps on his body.

She tipped her head to the side, exposing more of the slim column of her throat. He nibbled, laved and kissed the delicate skin until she trembled.

With his hands still holding hers captive, he brought their intertwined fingers together up her hips and across her tummy. Slowly moving over her heated flesh to below her belly button, he dipped teasingly beneath the edge of cherry-colored lace. He stilled their hands as her eyes widened and her breath caught.

"I know you're not ashamed of your body." He eased their joined hands lower to sift through the blond curls hidden beneath her underwear. "Show me what you like, babe. Tell me how you want to be pleasured."

She leaned against him, her bottom wedged tightly against his groin. The thoroughly sexy sight of her hands locked with his inching closer to her dewy center had him gritting his teeth. The intense pain and insistent throbbing of his erection made the idea of maintaining his control for much longer laughable.

The desire simmering in his veins turned hot and molten as together they explored her slick, moist folds. A deep groan of pure pleasure filled the air around them and he had no idea which of them had uttered the sound.

Her soft gaze filled with passion and remained transfixed on their reflection. Her lips parted and the breath eased out of her with a sensual rush of sound. Control slipped from his grasp. Need clawed him sharply. If he didn't make her his soon, he'd go insane.

He pushed her further, reaching deeper to open her and accompany her on an exploration of a different level. "What do you feel, Jana?" He felt ready to come out of his skin and wasn't sure how much longer he could last.

"Wet," she whispered. She arched her back. "Swollen and wet."

The combination of the warm flesh of her behind and delicate lace rasped against his erection. "So wet," he murmured against her ear. Together they exposed the center of her, then pushed her even higher. "So hot."

She whimpered as her body instantly contracted around the erotic invasion. "More?" he whispered in her ear.

"More." She cried out as he answered her sensual demand. Her desperate plea tested his limits.

Using the pad of his thumb, he sought her most sensitive place and teased her closer to ultimate fulfillment. Her hips pressed downward, seeking more, needing more. Her breath came in short, hard pants as the tension in her body drew tighter.

"Don't close your eyes," he gently ordered her. "Watch yourself."

"Don't...don't stop," she demanded, her voice strained. A deep cry followed as she tensed, then flew apart. The pants of breath coalesced into high-pitched moans of total ecstasy. His control took a swan dive off the side of a cliff as her body exploded around their interlaced fingers, and she witnessed the awe and wonder in her own reflection.

He didn't allow her body to cool, but turned her around and stripped off her panties before he lifted her so she could wrap her legs around his hips. Cupping her bottom in his hands, he pushed her back up against the wall, then guided her hot, moist heat down his rock-hard shaft until he was buried deep inside her.

She called out his name in a way that was purely primal and so filled with lust the sound shattered the wall surrounding his heart like a battering ram. She was totally and completely his, and he wouldn't have it any other way.

Her fingers were like tiny knives digging relentlessly into his shoulders, but he never registered pain. Only pleasure. She could have ripped him to shreds and it wouldn't have stopped him from guiding her hips harder, deeper down the length of his erection.

The last shred of his restraint crumbled. All that mattered was Jana and the beautiful intensity of the fierce giving and taking of their bodies and their hearts.

"Yes," she hissed, then yelled his name so loud and free of inhibition he felt it reverberate through him. She shuddered around him, her feminine sheath clenching so tight, each contraction touched his soul. A fierce groan ripped from his chest and he thrust into her one last time, coming in a hot rush.

He rested his forehead against hers as the world slowly righted itself. Slowly, his senses resumed a semblance of normal function. The ringing in his ears stilled. The sound of her labored breathing penetrated the remnants of lust-induced fog. Or were those haggard breaths coming from him? He didn't know and he didn't care.

"Please tell me you're on the Pill," he managed once he caught his breath. He'd totally lost control, and although safety wasn't an issue between them, he'd have only himself to blame for making love to her without the benefit of birth control.

"Yes," she whispered.

The scent of their lovemaking registered, filling him with contentment now that she'd set his mind at ease.

With their sated bodies still linked intimately together, he lifted his head and opened his eyes. His body instantly flexed the second he caught sight of their reflection in the mirror.

Her gaze met his and a weak smile turned up her mouth. "You've got to be kidding me." Humor laced her voice that had gone slightly hoarse. "I can barely breathe and you're ready to go again."

"Dammit, I love you," he said without thinking.

A slight frown creased her brow suddenly. Wariness filled her eyes as she regarded him carefully.

Alarm coursed through him. *What the hell did I just say?* His heart thumped heavily in his chest. He had *not* used the *L* word. He hadn't.

"Like this," he added hastily.

She gave him a slow, gentle smile, chasing the caution from her gaze. "Like this how?"

Carefully, he untangled their limbs and eased her to the floor. "Pleasured," he finally answered. "Very pleasured." But that wasn't completely true. Yes, he loved to see her sated, but...

She unhooked her bra, folded it neatly and set it on the luggage rack. "I'm going to take a shower." She scooped up her panties and folded them, then walked into the bathroom. "Join me?" she asked, glancing over her shoulder.

"No," he said. He wasn't referring to her invitation, but the realization that his feelings for her obliterated a lifelong belief. He did possess a heart after all, and it'd taken Jana to go and steal it for him to realize he wasn't emotionally bankrupt.

She shrugged, closed the door and the next thing he heard was the sound of running water. He couldn't breathe. Hell, he couldn't move. Shock did that to a guy.

Why? When? How?

Easy, he thought, as his heart rate calmed a fraction. Because she made it so simple to love her. The way her eyes danced with laughter, her easy smiles. How his heart always took an extra beat when her entire face lit up whenever she looked at him, even after he'd done something to tick her off. The way she refused to be bullied or let him have his way if it conflicted with her own wants, needs and desires. How she never hesitated to tell him when she thought he was wrong. He'd be a gray-haired old man before he could name each and every reason loving Jana was so damned easy.

So what was he supposed to do now? Deal with it and move on had been his method of coping for too many years for him to ignore. He couldn't come up with a single reason why his m.o. should alter just because he'd let Jana into his heart. He had to deal with his feelings for her, and together they would move on to whatever came next.

He walked into the bathroom and yanked the shower curtain aside. "No," he said to her again, determined she understand exactly what he'd meant.

She pulled her head out from under the spray of water. "I heard you the first time." A frown creased her forehead when he refused to relinquish the shower curtain. "Do you mind? That air is cold."

He stepped over the side of the tub and slid the curtain back. "I don't love you *like this.*" His heart started thumping again and his hand actually trembled when he reached up to cup her cheek. God, he'd never been more nervous in his life. "I love you, Jana."

No frown. No wariness. Just a heart-stopping smile as she leaned forward to brush her mouth over his in a feathery kiss.

"I love you, too." She scooped the bar of soap from the holder and handed it to him. "But you're still not off the hook for scaring me half to death this afternoon."

The woman certainly knew how to extract mileage out of a grudge. "Okay," he said and crossed his arms. "What *is* it going to take?"

Her eyes danced with laughter. "There is that back rub you've been promising me."

"That could lead to other things, you know."

She narrowed the distance between them and slid her arms around him, her fingers pressing into his backside to urge him closer. "I adore a man who plans ahead."

"HE DID WHAT?"

Ben's thunderous voice startled Jana out of a deep sleep. She bolted upright, wondering what had caused him to bellow like a ferocious bear.

"You can't be serious." A string of ripe curses followed. "I am not yelling," he shouted into the receiver.

Yeah. Sounded like a whisper to her.

He sat on the edge of the bed with his feet planted on the floor and his back facing her. She didn't need to see his face to understand he was furious about something. The extreme tenor of his voice and the tension radiating from him were pretty solid clues.

"Why are you calling me instead of Drew?" he asked whoever was on the other end. "Don't be a smart-ass, Cale, just answer me."

More ripe curses. Inventive ones, too.

"Yeah, whatever," he snapped harshly.

Jana scooted off the bed and quietly crept into the bathroom. They only had a few hours left alone before they drove to L.A. together. They'd planned to visit the aquarium and Cannery Row in Monterey this afternoon. Since he obviously needed at least the illusion of privacy, she decided to shower and dress.

"And I'm supposed to be happy about it?" she heard him shout before she turned on the shower.

She stepped beneath the spray once the water heated to her satisfaction. She could still hear his voice, but the words were indecipherable now. Having been up close and personal with his temper herself, she couldn't help but feel a stab of pity for whoever had disappointed him. And that, she realized suddenly, was his biggest flaw. Ben had dozens of exemplary qualities, with the exception of a shortage of coping skills when other people failed to live up to the expectations he had for them. Something she understood all too well having been there herself.

Spending time alone with Ben had been absolutely wonderful, and ranked high on her list of most incredible and memorable experiences. He loved her. Not just physically, but with his heart. She'd known how much it had cost him to tell her, too. The sheer terror on his face when those three little words had slipped out had been a dead giveaway.

She'd played it cool and hadn't let on that he hadn't fooled her with that panicked *like this* addendum. Although she had wondered if the words he'd blurted had been one of those caught-up-in-the-moment declarations he'd regret later. As her mother had constantly drilled into her and her sisters, a man would say just about anything if it involved sex, so the possibility existed.

She had no idea what the future held. Sure, they loved each other, but what came next, if anything? This morning had been the first time she'd ever woken up with him. Although she could definitely grow accustomed to having him in bed beside her, they were nowhere near ready to start shopping for china patterns. They weren't even close to considering cohabitation as the next logical step in their relationship.

By the time she stepped from the shower, the angry outbursts had stopped. She wrapped a towel around her wet hair, then another around her body and left the bathroom. Her heart sank to the pit of her stomach. The closet door stood open, with four empty hangers rocking back and forth on the bar.

She walked as far as the edge of the wall, then propped her shoulder against the cool plaster. In the time it'd taken her to clean up, he'd finished his phone call, dressed and had started packing.

"Change of plans?" she asked, unable to keep the disappointment from her voice.

He stuffed the shirts inside the canvas bag without bothering to fold them. The jeans and khakis suffered the same fate. "I'm sorry I woke you," he said shortly.

She was more sorry to see him packing. And walking out on her—again. "Something happen at work?" Her disappointment segued into a perfect rendition of resentment.

Which he caught. "Does it make a difference?" He chucked his shaving kit into the bag and looked up at her. His pale-blue eyes were as icy cold as his voice.

She pushed off the wall and shrugged. "I don't know," she answered honestly. The call had been from his brother, but considering they worked together, it was entirely possible Ben was leaving because of his job. "Maybe."

He regarded her dispassionately for a few more seconds. Was it her imagination, or did she really feel him starting to slip away from her? She had no idea how to stop him, or if she should even try.

"It's my brother," he finally said. He yanked the zipper of his bag closed.

"Drew?" she asked, instantly concerned. "Is he all right?"

"No," he snapped at her. "He's out of his friggin' mind."

Thoroughly confused, she dropped to the edge of the bed near the canvas bag. "Ben, what's going on?"

He let out a harsh breath and rammed his fingers through his hair. "He's married," he said without an ounce of warmth. "I knew he'd picked out a ring. I expected to hear he was engaged, not married. And not like this."

It seemed to her he should be celebrating, not storming around like a petulant child who didn't get his way.

"I don't mean to be obtuse, but I don't understand why you're so upset. I would think you'd be happy for him."

He narrowed his gaze. "You sound like Cale." From the rough tone of his voice, she didn't think he'd just paid her a compliment. "Why should I be happy that Drew blew off his responsibilities? He was supposed to take the fire detectives exam yesterday."

Men were too thick-headed for their own good. "Ben, your brother eloped. That's something to celebrate."

He gave her a look that clearly questioned her mental state. "Celebrate?"

"He can always take the exam later. Besides," she added, "if you knew he was planning to ask this woman to marry him, what's the big deal?"

"The big deal is he ran off like he had something to hide."

Thick *and* dense. "Eloping isn't about hiding anything." She smiled as she rose from the bed. "Eloping is all about being so in love that you can't wait to start your life together."

His frown deepened. Obviously he didn't share her romantic views on the subject. "He has responsibilities."

She crossed the room to the dresser and pulled open the drawer. "To who?" she asked, dropping the towel and slipping into a pair of navy-blue cotton panties. "You?"

She ignored him as she fastened the matching bra, then dug a thick navy sweater from the next drawer and pulled it over her head. "Oh, my God," she said, disentangling the towel she'd forgotten was still wrapped around her hair. "That's what this is all about, isn't it? You're ticked because Drew didn't tell *you* he was eloping."

He crossed his arms over his chest and glared at her, his expression thunderous. Uh-oh. She'd hit a nerve. With precise accuracy, too.

She let out a sigh and moved toward him. "Ben, your brother is a grown man."

"I know that," he said. "I helped get him there."

She laid her hand over his arm, but he didn't respond to her touch. He just continued to glare at her, the expression in his eyes so glacial she fought off a shiver.

"He doesn't need your permission to get married." She dropped her hand to her side. "Whether or not he takes some test is his business now. It's not your job to control his life any longer."

"I never said I wanted to control his life."

"Not in so many words. Look, I do get it. You were forced into a position where you had to look out for your brothers, and I respect that. You were just a kid, yet you held their lives together by assuming responsibility for them. You didn't have a choice then. But you do now. It's time for you to let go and allow them to grow."

He spun away from her and stormed across the room to the window. "You don't know what you're talking about." Just because he kept his back to her didn't alleviate the deep chill in his words. Or the warning that she'd ventured into treacherous terrain.

She'd never backed down from his blustering before, and she wasn't about to start now. "Oh, I think I do," she told him. "If you keep everything under control, then nothing can fall apart. Well guess what? The world won't stop spinning if you let go of it for once."

He looked over his shoulder at her, then turned to face her completely. "There's only one control freak in this room. I'm not the one who keeps the contents of my fridge alphabetized."

She folded her arms and tilted her hip to the side. Then she threw in a narrow-eyed glare for good measure. "Oh, now *there's* an intelligent response. Don't you dare bite my head off because I've brought up something you're unwilling to face."

"You weren't there, Jana. You don't know what it was like."

"Maybe I don't, but I know that your big speech of dealing with it and moving on is a load of bull. And I thought *I* had baggage. *You*'ve got a steamer trunk full of it." She let him stew on that for a minute while she went to the closet for her jeans.

After she shrugged into the heavy denim, she walked toward him. "You know, Ben, this goes way beyond older-sibling syndrome. You think if you're in control then things can't fall apart? Well, life just doesn't work that way. We don't have that kind of power."

"You're wrong," he said.

"I don't think so," she argued. "Your dad still died, Ben. You were in control, but you couldn't save him, even from himself. When are you going to forgive yourself for something that wasn't even your fault?"

Fury burned in his gaze. "Don't push me, Jana," he warned coldly.

She was ready to push his stubborn hide out the window. At least he was fighting with her and not shutting her out where she couldn't attempt to make him see more clearly. "You wanted me off the investigation because you were afraid I'd tell you that you hadn't been in control of the situation. You *were* in control, and Fitz still died. How long are you going to carry that one around?"

A muscle ticked in his jaw. He looked as if he wanted to stuff a sock in her mouth just to shut her up—or maybe throw *her* out the window.

He stormed to the bed and grabbed the canvas bag. "I have to go."

She followed him to the door. "And do what?" she sniped at him. "Punish Drew by taking away his TV privileges for a week because he was a naughty boy?"

He slowly turned toward her. "Be careful, Jana," he said, his tone low and filled with a warning she couldn't possibly mistake. "You won't like it if I push back."

Her patience with him reached the limit, then snapped like a dry twig. "Why did you even bother to come here if all you're going to do is run out the first chance you get?"

He dropped the canvas bag with a dull thud. "Because," he said, leaning toward her until they were practically nose to nose, "I was ordered to take time off."

She held her ground. "Oh? So what are you saying? I was a convenient substitute? A diversion?"

He stared at her, his eyes so cold and hard, she almost wished he'd start blustering again. Anything to let her know he felt something.

His silence ripped her heart to shreds.

"You bastard," she fired at him. "I will not be a convenience for you or any man." God, she almost wished he hadn't told her he'd loved her. Maybe then she could breathe.

He shrugged, then stooped to pick up his bag before turning and tugging open the door.

"Dammit, Ben. Stay here and finish this."

Nothing in his eyes as he looked over his shoulder at her on the way out the door resembled the warm, caring man she'd fallen so helplessly in love with.

"We *are* finished," he said, before he walked out of her life.

14

It took Ben just under six hours to make the drive from Carmel to L.A. By the time he pulled up in front of Cale and Amanda's place in Hermosa Beach, the sun had already begun to set on the horizon, casting long shadows on the house. His temper cooled on the long drive, which made way for a nagging conscience branded with the image of Jana's eyes filling with a deep pain. He'd been a fool. He'd let her believe she was no more important to him than a convenient roll in the hay.

It'd taken three-hundred-plus miles for him to realize nothing could be further from the truth.

Provided she'd even speak to him again, he had some serious apologizing ahead of him. But now that she'd finally been acquainted with the cold-hearted bastard he really could be, he expected her to tell him exactly where to go, and what he could do once he got there.

She might have pushed hard on a hot button he hadn't realized existed, but he accepted full responsibility for his behavior. Why hadn't she just let him be? He would've come back to L.A., dealt with Drew, and everything would have been fine between them. Instead, she'd pushed him to the limit of his patience. She'd prodded until she'd unearthed things better left buried, then dragged them out and poked some more.

She'd not only found the scar of a wound he'd thought healed years ago, she'd sliced it open, then stood back to watch him bleed.

He cut the engine and left his truck parked in the sloped drive behind Drew's SUV. Amanda's new convertible was missing, which probably meant that only his brothers were waiting for him.

Waiting for him to what? Tell Drew what a mistake he'd made because he'd blown off something as important as his career? That he wasn't ready for marriage and an instant family? Or maybe, Ben thought suddenly, Jana was right. The reason he'd really driven back to L.A. in record time was because Drew had made a life-altering decision without consulting him first, meaning he was no longer needed.

He walked toward the rear of the house without any concrete answers. All he did know was that he didn't have the energy for another emotional battle. He was still recovering from the last one only hours ago.

He pushed through the gate to the backyard. Pearl, Cale's black Lab mix, greeted him by barreling around the side of the house, barking excitedly until he bent down to pet her. "At least someone's happy to see me," he told the dog, then gave her thick side a hearty rub.

Cale waited for him on the covered patio. "You look like hell."

Made sense, Ben thought, because he sure felt that way. He hadn't bothered to shave, just packed his gear, stomped all over Jana's pride, then walked out on her.

"Hello to you, too," he groused at Cale. For once,

Cale kept his mouth shut. Maybe Amanda had taught him some manners.

Pearl trotted into the house ahead of them, found her giant stuffed pillow and made a few circles before finally settling down with a gusty groan. Cale's fixer-upper had come a long way. The house had always been comfortable, but there was a more welcoming feel to it now, which Ben credited to Amanda's touch.

Framed movie posters and other film memorabilia decorated the walls of the recently remodeled den. He spied a new addition, a framed page from a movie script, autographed by one of the starring actors. Circling a square coffee table were a pair of matching sofa recliners and a leather chair, arranged for optimum viewing in front of the big-screen television.

He attempted to shoo one of the black-and-white cats from the chair, but the feline meowed at him in protest, refusing to budge. "Stubborn female," he muttered, then dropped wearily on one of the sofas. "Where's Drew?" he asked Cale.

"Upstairs." Cale sat on the other sofa and stretched his arms along the back. "He'll be down in a minute."

Several books and a spiral binder filled with notes littered the coffee table. He picked up one of the books and looked at his brother. "Hot Sex and How to Do It Right Every Time?" he read aloud. "Amanda branching out from suspense novels?"

"Research," Cale said, then grinned. "It's for her next book. An erotic thriller."

Amanda had been one of Cale's strays. She'd been in the wrong place at the wrong time when a paint-and-wallpaper-supply warehouse had caught fire. She'd had amnesia, caused by a head injury, and Cale had taken her in until she recovered her memory, which had returned in the guise of the main character of the novel she'd been researching.

Ben set the how-to manual back on the table and managed a half-hearted chuckle. "Knowing the way she absorbs her research, I don't think I want to know any more," he told his brother. "I didn't see her car."

A scruffy orange ball of fluff sprang over the arm of the sofa to land in Cale's lap. "She and Tilly took Emily over to Debbie's." Cale winced and eased the cat to the cushion when she tried to use his legs to sharpen her claws. "Something about an indoctrination for Emily's first girls' night in."

Sounded more like Amanda was protecting Emily—from him. He had nothing against Emily. He hardly knew her, something that would be remedied now that she'd married Drew.

Drew came down the stairs and walked into the den. He carried a plastic bottle of soda in one hand and two bottles of beer in the other.

"Tilly ever tell you what they do over there?" Cale asked, taking the beer Drew handed him.

"Not really. Eat chocolate. Paint their toenails. OD on chick flicks all night." Drew shrugged. "They could dance naked under the moon for all we know." He handed Ben a chilled amber bottle. "Thought you might like a cold one after such a long drive."

Ben nodded his thanks. He set the unopened bottle

on the table and stood, extending his hand to his brother. "Congratulations, Drew."

Drew shook his brother's hand, although caution filled his eyes. "Thanks."

Ben couldn't help but notice that, whether consciously or not, Drew had chosen to sit near Cale. A united front, he thought. Against him.

"You should have told me you were getting married," he said to Drew. He tried not to sound as if he was lecturing, but he couldn't completely mask the censure in his tone.

Cale twisted the cap off his beer. "What's the point of eloping if you announce it to everyone?"

"Not everyone," Ben said. He glanced at Cale, then shifted his attention back to Drew. "Your family."

A family that had grown in the past year, and would continue to grow as Cale and Amanda, and now Drew and Emily, started families of their own. A sharp pang pierced his heart. So where did that leave him?

Drew propped his foot over his knee and gave him a level stare. "Emily and I decided to elope because she's already starting to show. With the opening of her new ad agency scheduled for the first of the year, and the baby due late March, when were we supposed to plan a wedding?"

Ben looked hard at his youngest brother. "Couldn't you have waited a week?" he asked him. "At least then you wouldn't have blown off the exam."

"So I'll take it in six months when it's offered again." Drew shrugged. "Even if I pass, I still have to wait for an opening and go through the interview process."

"But you'll have priority," Ben reminded him. "It could be a year or more before you make detective now." Drew had a rare talent for reading a burn, and Ben hated to see him waste it. "You're really willing to wait that long?"

"If it takes a year, it takes a year," Drew said impatiently. "I don't care if it takes two years. Emily is what matters. She's more important to me than leaving arson for the fire detective's squad."

Ben wanted to understand his brother's reasoning, but he couldn't grasp why Drew was so willing to put his career on hold. The elopement made sense, although Ben still would've preferred to have been informed beforehand. So he could've tried to change Drew's mind? Or had he gone off the deep end today because he didn't want to face the truth—that his brothers no longer needed him?

Ben looked over at Cale. "You haven't said much."

"If he wants to wait a year to defect to the other side and become a blue canary, that's his business. Drew and Emily have to make that decision," Cale said, his gaze intent. "I know I'd never make a career move like that without first talking it over with Amanda."

"It's going to be hard enough on Em with a new baby and starting her own ad agency," Drew added. "Changing jobs now would make it a lot harder on her. I'd be looking at long hours and I can't do that to her when she's going to need me to be there for her."

"What about your responsibility to yourself?" Ben asked him. "What about what you want?"

"Emily and the baby are my responsibility. I want what's best for them."

Ben let out a sigh and leaned back against the cushion. He scrubbed his hand down his face and didn't bother to remind Drew that he'd sacrificed his chance to become a fire detective for a kid that wasn't even his. Apparently the baby's paternity made little difference to his brother.

Emily had been pregnant when she and Drew had met. The father, Emily's ex-boyfriend, lived in New York. Drew had told Ben recently that Emily and the father still hadn't made any firm decisions regarding visitation and custody. Surely his brother had to realize the problems they could be facing.

"What about what's best for you?" he asked Drew.

Drew's bright-green eyes hardened with determination. "You're my brother, and I love and respect you. God only knows what would've happened if you hadn't been there for us. But Emily is my wife, Ben. If you can't accept that..."

"I don't object to your marriage," he told Drew wearily, and he meant it. He'd already alienated one person he loved today, and that was one too many. "I'm only worried you've taken on more than you realize, and given up a whole lot more."

Drew set his bottle of soda on the table with a sharp click. "That's not your job anymore." He shot off the sofa, his eyes glittering with frustration. "In case you haven't looked around lately, Cale and I have been taking care of ourselves for a while now."

Drew walked to the sliding-glass door. For a minute,

Ben thought he'd leave, but he braced his arm above his head on the doorjamb and stared into the backyard.

The world won't stop spinning if you let go of it for once.

Drew's argument and Jana's words slammed into him like a freight train. They were both right, he realized reluctantly. He *was* trying to hold on—desperately. Not because looking out for his brothers was all he knew, but if he held on a little tighter this time, if he kept them even closer, then just maybe he'd be able to keep them safe. But, as Jana had bluntly pointed out, life simply didn't work that way. He really didn't have that kind of power. Maybe the time had come for him to let go and stop assuming responsibility for things he had no control over.

Just because Drew had run off to get married without consulting him first didn't have to mean he was losing his brother, either. His relationship with Cale hadn't changed when he'd married Amanda a few weeks ago. Losing his brothers wasn't what had him running scared; it was the fear of no longer having a purpose in their lives.

Cale set his beer on the table and looked over his shoulder at Drew. "Let me see if I can put this in terms even he might understand."

Drew glanced in their direction, his expression skeptical. "Good luck."

"Being married is like being on a team." Cale propped his bare feet on the edge of the coffee table. "But instead of eleven guys on a football field, or a squad of firefighters, there's only two of you on this team. When a save is made on the job, the whole team gets the credit. When there's a problem, the team pulls together to find a solution. Marriage is that way, too. You work together."

Drew came back to the sofa and sat. "That was good," he said to Cale.

"Thanks." Cale grinned. "I do have my moments."

Ben didn't know whether to strangle the two of them or laugh. "Okay," he said in defeat. "I get it. I'm only concerned about your future, Drew. I know how much you wanted to make the move."

"The job will be there when the time is right for me," Drew answered.

Cale laced his fingers behind his head. "There's more to life than work, Ben. I heard Rick had to threaten you with a suspension to get you to take some time off."

Both of his brothers looked at him with concern. "If you burn out, then what do you have?" Drew asked him.

"You know, you're not the only one in this family who worries," Cale added.

This wasn't supposed to be about him. And he certainly didn't like that his brothers were worried about him, either.

"Keep it up, and you'll end up with a forced retirement," Cale warned him. "Then what are you going to do? Hang out with the tribal elders and guzzle coffee all day?"

"At his age?" Drew winced. "Now that would be pathetic."

"Okay, I get the point," Ben said. The tribal elders were retired firefighters who spent much of their time hanging around the firehouse. Most spewed words of wisdom and offered sage advice. They were respected and revered by the actives for their experience and years of service. Ben was far too young to join the tribe, and he didn't want to waste his life reliving glory days over bad cups of coffee because that was all he had. "I'll work on getting a life. Happy?"

"Why don't you get yourself a *wife*," Drew suggested. "Let someone take care of you for a change."

"That OSHA babe's a hottie," Cale said, then exchanged a blatant, conspiratorial look with Drew.

"Who will probably never speak to me again," Ben admitted. Which was more than he deserved after the way he'd treated her.

Cale chuckled. "Showed her your winning personality, didn't you?"

"Something like that," Ben muttered. He straightened and snagged the beer from the table. Twisting off the cap, he took a long drink.

"Well?" Drew prompted impatiently.

"We had an argument." Because she was stubborn, infuriating, and she insisted on dragging the demons out of the closet to prove they were still there after all. She wanted him to resurrect a past he'd already buried, because she'd known he'd never fully laid it to rest. Although he'd only been a kid, he'd dealt with the loss of his parents and the aftermath in an adult manner. There was a world of difference, he realized, and that was something he planned to correct immediately.

Cale shook his head. "Uh-uh," he said. "No way. You

don't argue. You try to bully me and Drew around, but when it comes to women, you're tighter than a virgin."

"He argues with her," Drew told Cale.

Cale let out a low whistle. "Wow," he said, his blue eyes widening in surprise. "This really *is* serious."

Ben did not appreciate his brothers speculating about his relationship with Jana as if he weren't even in the room. "Butt out," he warned them. They didn't even glance his way.

"You missed them in action at the firehouse," Drew continued. "We could hear them shouting all the way upstairs. You know, she might even have a temper quicker to fire than Amanda's."

Because she's so passionate, Ben thought. About everything. When Jana believed in something, or someone, she allowed her passionate nature to rule her. She relied on her instincts, and she didn't believe in holding back either. All of which translated to a never-ending roller-coaster ride, filled with ups, downs and every possible emotion in between. Life with her would never be boring.

Life without her would be damned lonely.

"You aren't looking so good." The concern in Cale's voice dragged Ben away from his miserable thoughts. "Is it that bad?"

Ben drained the last of his beer and set the empty bottle on the table. If Jana was there, she'd flip because he hadn't used a coaster. "She thinks she's a convenience," he said. "I didn't say anything to change her mind."

At least Drew had the decency to show a modicum of

sympathy. Until he started laughing. "You are so screwed."

Cale didn't bother with compassion. "He won't be anytime soon," he said with a hearty laugh.

"Groveling helps," Drew offered, looking a little too sheepish. Memories of his own mistakes he'd made with Emily, no doubt.

"Flowers are good," Cale added, "but I think this calls for jewelry, old man."

Drew dug into his hip pocket and pulled out his wallet. He extracted a business card and slid it across the table. "You're going to need this."

Ben picked up the card. "A jeweler?"

"No lingerie," Cale's voice held a distinct warning. "Whatever you do, don't give a woman anything that makes her think you want sex when she's ticked off at you."

"Big mistake," Drew agreed.

Ben wasn't accustomed to admitting he'd been wrong, nor was he used to receiving advice from his brothers. That'd always been his role. Today, he was grateful for their expertise.

"You think it might work?" He'd try anything if it meant having Jana back in his life.

Cale and Drew shared a smile, as if they were privy to a private joke—and he was the punch line.

"What do you have to lose?" Drew's grin widened. "Other than your pride."

15

"ALL OF THIS stuff is from him?" Chloe plucked one of the two red velvet jeweler's boxes still sitting on Jana's dining table and opened it.

"Oh, Jana." Lauren trailed an airbrushed fingernail over the emerald-and-diamond tennis bracelet Chloe held up for inspection. "It's absolutely stunning."

Even Chloe managed to look impressed when she opened the box containing the pair of matching earrings. "He is seriously sucking up."

Jana carried the vase of autumn flowers to the sink to add water. She had no idea where she'd even put this newest arrival. Her apartment was already crammed full of elaborate floral arrangements and thick, leafy plants she couldn't even begin to name. "It's starting to look like a funeral parlor in here," she said. "He isn't exactly subtle, is he?"

When Ben had realized she wasn't going to take his calls, the gifts had started arriving. He'd had them delivered to her office, her apartment, even on-site when she'd been in the field yesterday conducting a routine follow-up inspection with one of her new team members at another firehouse in the valley. In addition to all the flowers, exquisite jewelry, gourmet chocolates and desserts arrived, sometimes two or three times a day.

By Wednesday she'd started bringing home the flower arrangements, strictly out of embarrassment. Even her new assistant, Paul, had started giving her a hard time because she refused to take Ben's phone calls.

"This is all a very nice touch," Lauren said, "but has he apologized for acting like a donkey wanker?"

Jana laughed abruptly. After the miserable week she'd had, Lauren's brash assessment helped lighten her mood. After filling the vase, she left the flower arrangement in the sink and walked back to the table where the three of them had just finished off an impromptu Sunday brunch.

She reached over Lauren's shoulder and snagged a thick stack of pink message slips. "Several times," Jana told them. "To my new assistant, who has started referring to Ben as the Dreamboat. I'm surprised he didn't bribe the parking attendant to put messages on my car." She let go and the message slips slid from her fingers, raining over the table in a pink shower. "If I had an answering machine instead of voice mail, I'd have to buy a new tape, because he would've worn it out by now."

"Good grief, Jana," Chloe exclaimed, inspecting the bracelet to see if it was real. "He sends you jewelry and you haven't returned his calls?"

Lauren stood and circled the table to place her hand over Chloe's forehead, which Chloe promptly slapped away. "What's wrong with you?"

Lauren smiled down at a frowning Chloe. "Just checking for fever."

"Bite me, Lauren," Chloe said impatiently. "Jana,

you have to forgive him sooner or later. What are you waiting for? A Ferrari?"

"I refuse to be a convenience for any man." Even for one she loved. *Especially* for one she loved.

"You are being more stubborn than usual," Lauren pointed out as she returned to her seat.

Her downfall, Jana knew, but she really didn't have a choice. She didn't trust her willpower. Hearing his deep, rich voice on her voice mail was hard enough. One look in those impossible blue eyes, or a tilt of his wickedly sexy smile and she'd cave.

"Why is it so wrong for me to want someone that values me as a person? Am I supposed to wait until he decides when it's right? You know the kind of relationship my parents had. My mother lived her life according to my father's schedule, and what did she get in return? An unfaithful husband who rarely remembered he even had a family. I refuse to live that way."

Lauren lifted the lid on the enormous box of Godiva chocolates that had arrived that morning. "You haven't even opened them."

"Go for it," Jana said, smiling at Lauren's disappointment at finding the box untouched. "Take them home with you." *He'll probably send more anyway,* she thought.

Chloe leaned back in the chair and crossed her arms. "It doesn't have to be that way," she said. "He screwed up, but take a good look around. I think he figured it out."

The distinct tone of the instant messaging program from her laptop computer bleeped, stilling the argument hovering on Jana's lips. She'd been online earlier looking up the recipe for seafood quiche to make for brunch. She'd called her friends at the last minute because she couldn't bear the idea of spending another moment miserable and alone. She'd been rushed for time and had apparently forgotten to shut down her laptop.

Another bleep had Lauren tipping her chair closer to the computer stand for a better look at the laptop. "Uh-oh." She laughed. "You've got mail."

Chloe got up to stand behind Lauren. "FireBen?" She looked at Jana and giggled. "His handle is FireBen?"

"He is a firefighter," she reminded Chloe, hating that she'd sounded so defensive. Personally, she thought his handle was kinda cute. Corny, but still cute. "What does he want now?"

"Aw," Lauren pointed to the screen and cooed. "It says, *Please talk to me.*"

Chloe snagged Jana's hand and pulled her out of her chair. "Come on, Jana," she said, guiding Jana to the computer stand. "You are going to talk to him. You can't make him suffer forever. You're not that heartless."

She was too that heartless. Her heart no longer existed since he'd stolen it, then cruelly smashed it into unrecognizable fragments.

If she didn't have a heart, then why did she still hurt so much? Because she loved him, she thought. Not with her heart, but clear down to her soul.

"Oh all right," she muttered. "But I'm doing this under protest."

Chloe pointed to the laptop. "Type."

Bored? She entered the word in the reply box. Befor
she chickened out, she clicked the send button.

Be nice.

Jana muttered a curse. You want nice, message an
other girl.

I miss you.

She missed him, too, so much that she ached. But tha
didn't mean she would let him batter her self-esteem
second time.

Too bad for you. She clicked Send.

Come see me.

Not a chance.

Still mad, huh?

She drummed her fingers on the keyboard and trie
to find the right word. *Seething.*

I love you.

"Ooh, the man is positively infuriating," she com
plained. "Not a word," she warned her friends whe
they started with all that gooey "Aw" stuff again.

She clicked on the pull-down menu, moved th
mouse over the little yellow happy-face icon with a bi
yawn and hit the select button.

"Jana, don't," Lauren said. "That's mean."

She glanced over her shoulder and grinned as she h
the send button.

Within seconds, *I want you* popped up on the screen

Dozens of sexy images immediately flooded he
mind. Exciting, sensual memories of the incredibl
pleasures they'd shared. A sorry substitute for the real
ity she knew could be hers if she'd be inclined to lowe

her standards and accept whatever meager scraps he'd throw her way when the mood struck.

"He doesn't know when to quit," she muttered. She typed *Take a cold shower.*

No fun—alone.

"Oooh, I do like the way he thinks," Chloe drawled.

"You would," Lauren teased her.

Jana giggled. *$50 + red light district = fun—at your convenience.*

BEN WINCED at Jana's reply. *Ouch!* he typed.

Another smiley face appeared on the monitor, this one with a halo above its head. Emily and Amanda both started giggling. "I think I'm really going to like her," Amanda said from over his shoulder.

Emily leaned against the edge of Amanda's mahogany desk, her hand resting protectively over the slight bulge of her tummy. "You're not trying hard enough, Ben," she said. "Where's all that legendary Perry charm?"

He leaned back in the leather chair, prepared to admit defeat. "Drew got it all." When it came to women, he wished he had a fraction of his brother's charisma. "Tell me again why I let you two talk me into this?"

Emily looked at him as if he were dense. "Because you're in love with her."

"It'll work," Amanda encouraged him. "Just use your imagination."

"My imagination is going broke," he complained. He'd tried flowers, jewelry and chocolates at his sisters-in-law's insistence, but nothing had worked. Clearly they had grossly underestimated the extent of Jana's tenacity.

"You didn't send her lingerie, did you?"

"No," he told Emily.

"Good, because if she thinks you want sex, forget it."

"So I've heard," he muttered.

Amanda settled her hands on his shoulders and gave him a gentle shake. "Think, Ben. Think. What's the one thing you know she can't resist?"

"You know, I could take out a full-page ad in the *Times* for you," Emily offered. "I'll do the copy free of charge."

"There's a limit to my humiliation, Emily."

Amanda gave his shoulder a firm pat. "Not after what you did, there isn't."

Drew poked his head into Amanda's office. "Cale wants to know how many steaks to pick up at the store."

"Six," Ben told his brother, then turned back to the computer with renewed energy. If Jana wouldn't come to him willingly, he wasn't above dragging her—kicking and screaming if necessary. He'd show her tenacity. One way or another, they were going to resolve this mess—today.

I want to see you, he wrote. He should've just gone to her place as he'd wanted to and groveled as Drew had suggested. Instead, he'd listened to his sisters-in-law and was now embroiled in an electronic sparring match.

Blue is not your color, flashed on the monitor in response.

He shook his head, confused. "She lost me," he admitted.

"She's saying not to hold your breath," Emily explained, her voice tinged with laughter.

They could go on like this all day. "What did you say earlier?" he asked Amanda. "What can't Jana...what was it?"

"Resist." Amanda twisted her long auburn hair into a knot, then snatched a pencil from the holder on the desk and weaved it through her hair to hold it in place. "What's the one thing you know she absolutely cannot say no to?"

At one time, he'd arrogantly believed she couldn't resist him, but after the past week, she'd staunchly proven otherwise. He smiled suddenly, and typed, *Chicken?*

Never! Jana sent back.

He chuckled. "Wanna bet, babe?" he said as he typed his reply, hit Send and waited.

I DARE YOU!

Jana gasped when the words flashed on the screen, taunting her. Daring her.

Don't go there! She hit the send button so hard she broke her fingernail.

"Okay, that's it. Drama over," Lauren stood and slung her big canvas bag over her shoulder. "Let's go, Chloe. She's officially history."

"You can't leave me," she pleaded.

I double dare you.

Jana panicked. "Don't go." If her friends deserted

her, she'd do something stupid, like take him up on that stupid dare. "He's not playing fair."

Chloe bent down and gave her a supportive hug. "You're in love with him. He obviously feels the same way. What if this is the real deal, Jana? Are you willing to risk it?"

The computer bleeped. She was afraid to look.

You know what's next...

Jana bit her lip and stared at the monitor. The cursor blinked, mocking her. Challenging her to pick up the gauntlet he'd thrown down unfairly.

"I'm afraid," she said quietly. "He's already hurt me once. What if he does it again? I don't know if I can handle it."

Lauren offered her a sympathetic smile. "The only thing that keeps us from what we want, Jana, is fear. If we conquer the fear, isn't the reward that much sweeter?"

She had a hard time arguing with Lauren's logic. Especially since she'd already had a taste of how sweet those rewards were. "If I don't risk anything, then there's nothing to gain. Right?"

"No pain, no gain," Chloe added.

"I've already felt the burn once," she reminded them. "Trust me, it isn't any fun."

"We're leaving." Lauren nudged Chloe toward the door. "Call if you need us."

Jana nodded and turned her attention back to the laptop.

"Twenty bucks says she's having make-up sex within the hour," she heard Chloe say before the door closed.

Jana drew in a deep breath and let it out slowly. And hesitated. "Risk it," she said. Two words that had completely changed her life a little over two weeks ago. She'd taken a chance once, and the results had been more than she'd ever dreamed possible.

You do not play fair. She clicked the send button again and prayed she wasn't making a mistake. One from which she might never recover.

THE FORTY-FIVE MINUTES he'd waited for Jana to arrive at Cale's had been the longest of his life. Now that she was here, he wasn't sure where to begin. She certainly wasn't going to make it easy on him, that much he did know.

She leaned against the front fender of her sporty coupe with her arms folded in front of her. A pair of dark sunglasses shielded her eyes from the sun, and prevented him from accurately gauging her mood.

In accordance with the unseasonably warm weather, she wore a little denim skirt that showed off the perfection of her long, shapely legs, and a bright-red top just short enough to allow him an enticing glimpse of her bare midriff when she moved. If she was wearing that drop-dead cherry-red lace combination beneath, he'd be a goner.

The warm breeze blew a lock of her hair into her face and she impatiently pushed it behind her ear. "This better be good," she sassed him. "I gave up a root canal to come here."

His lips twitched. "Dentists don't work on Sunday," he reminded her.

She slid her sunglasses down the slope of her nose, far enough to glare at him over the rim. "I was making a point."

So he'd figured. "I'm glad you decided to come."

One arched eyebrow winged up before she used the tip of her middle finger to push the sunglasses back in place.

He tried not to wince, but her message was pretty clear. "If I told you how sorry I am, will you forgive me?"

She flashed him one of those sugary smiles guaranteed to irritate him. But not today. If it killed him, he would not let his patience slip.

"Why?" she asked, taking off her sunglasses.

With her so close, the need to touch her tripled. He wanted to feel her curves pressed against him so badly he ached. If he wasn't afraid she'd literally do him bodily harm, he'd pull her into his arms and kiss her senseless until she forgot how angry she was with him for being a jackass.

The woman was definitely doing a number on his patience. But he hadn't survived hell because he lacked a determination that could put her stubbornness to shame.

He closed the space between them and leaned into her. Her eyes widened in surprise as he braced his hands on either side of her hips, trapping her between him and her car. "I love you, Jana," he said, once they were at eye level. "That has to count for something."

"You have such a way with words." The wariness

and hurt in her gaze defused her sarcastic taunt. "Too bad the ones you don't say get you into trouble."

"I have *never* thought of you as a convenience."

She closed her eyes and turned her head to the side, but not before he caught the glimpse of hope she tried to hide from him. He waited, and felt her resolve slowly weaken. The tense set of her shoulders eased.

For all of five seconds.

She made a sound of disgust and pushed past him. The distance she put between them was so much more than physical. He was going to lose her.

"That wasn't the impression you gave me." She tossed her sunglasses on the dashboard of her car before she faced him again, hurt and anger etched on her face. "It was fun while it lasted," she said and reached for the car door. "We need to accept that we're just not right for each other and move on."

Before she could open the door, he settled his hand over hers. She was wrong. If she truly wanted to move on, then her voice wouldn't have sounded so brittle, and her eyes wouldn't be filling with moisture.

"What do you want from me?" he asked her. "Tell me what I have to do because I'm running out of ideas here."

His chest tightened with dread when she slowly shook her head from side to side. Dammit, he knew she loved him, so why was she so eager to walk away? He'd screwed up, he knew that, but she wasn't even open to the possibility of giving him a second chance.

"I want what you can't give me," she whispered.

He smoothed the back of his hand down her cheek "You have my heart, Jana. Can't that be enough?"

She bit her lip and squeezed her eyes shut. He couldn't breathe.

"What if it isn't?" she asked as she opened her eyes "I'm not the kind of person that you can keep on a shel and only bring down when it's good for you. Since was a little girl I've known how it feels to be only sec ond best. It hurts. Please, Ben. Don't ask me to g through it again. I just can't do it."

Understanding slammed into him with the subtlet of a wrecking ball as he realized exactly how deepl he'd hurt her. Because he'd let her believe she hadn' mattered enough to him, he'd inadvertently awakene a dragon of her own that she hadn't slain. God, wh hadn't he seen it sooner? Her die-hard perfectionism Her reaction every time he walked out the door becaus he'd believed he was needed elsewhere. He'd walke all over her insecurities caused by a self-absorbed par ent, and he hadn't even known.

Too many years of taking charge made him instinc tively want to beat the beast back into its cave to protec her, but he knew he couldn't do it. Not this time. Sh had to conquer that demon herself so old wounds coul eventually heal. She wouldn't have to face it alone though, because if she'd let him, he'd be there, offering his support and encouragement, along with his love.

He cupped her cheeks in his hands and urged her t look at him. "You will *never* be an afterthought to me Jana. I promise you."

"I know I sound selfish—"

"No. Don't think that way. Selfish would be an ultimatum. You haven't demanded I give up my job or my family for you, have you?"

"I wouldn't ever ask you to give up something that's important to you."

He dipped his head and brushed his mouth across hers. "Then stop asking me to give up on you."

Her bottom lip trembled. He waited, but the tears never came. "I love you," she whispered softly. "So much it scares me."

"I know, babe," he said, pulling her into his embrace. "It scares me, too. But we'll figure it out. Okay?"

She nodded and gave him a tremulous smile as she wreathed her arms around his neck, bringing her body in perfect alignment with his. She clung to him as if she never wanted to let him go, and that was just fine by him.

He didn't care that they were standing in the middle of his brother's driveway, and gave in to the need to taste her. Desire rolled through his body with the force of a backdraft, hot and impossible to tame, until the blare of a horn brought an abrupt end to their kiss.

"I have to know something." He ushered Jana toward the rear of the house as Cale and Drew pulled into the driveway. "What are you wearing under that skirt?"

She walked ahead of him on the narrow concrete path, giving him a great view of her behind hugged in tight denim. "Wanna see?"

He snagged her hand and pulled her to him. The air hissed out between his teeth when she wiggled her bottom against him. He dipped his head and caught her earlobe between his teeth. "Tell me," he demanded, "and I'll know if you lie."

"Red," she whispered. "Lace. Like the color of ripe cherries."

He groaned in pure agony. "You don't play fair," he told her as she slipped away from him.

She turned to face him, a definite sassy glint in her eyes and a sinful smile curving her lush mouth. "I never intended to."

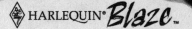
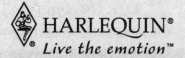

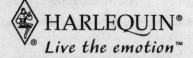